Dear Diary,

I honestly never thought my life could be this exciting and at the same time so worrying.

After months of hard work, my very own Forrester Square Day Care is up and running. It's a dream come true—my best friend, Hannah, as my business partner, a wonderful staff, adorable kids….

So why this sense of doom?

I guess it might have to do with Dad finally coming home from prison. Twenty years is a long time, and though none of us believed for one minute he was guilty, our family's going to have a lot of adjusting to do.

And then there's Drew. My little brother may be a successful architect now, but I'm not about to stop looking out for him, especially when a pregnant woman shows up on his doorstep!

I want to like Jeanie Shaw—but my radar is telling me her story about being in mortal danger is full of holes. Drew thinks my suspicions are groundless, of course, but then all he sees is a beautiful woman in distress, and her helpless baby.

I'm really trying to keep an open mind, but I don't want my brother hurt. If this Jeanie person is up to no good, she'll have me to deal with.

Till tomorrow,
Katherine

MURIEL JENSEN

is the award-winning author of over sixty books that tug at readers' hearts. She has won a Reviewer's Choice Award and a Career Achievement Award from *Romantic Times* magazine, and says she's had such a great time that it's almost embarrassing.

Muriel met her husband-to-be, Ron, at a Xerox machine at the *Los Angeles Times*. (There were two copiers in a *nine-story* building. That tells you how long ago it was.)

She always wanted to be a writer and sometimes helped out as a reporter at several small newspapers Ron edited. But Muriel soon learned that journalism was not for her—editors got really upset when you made up stuff—so she decided to stick to fiction.

Today, Muriel is best loved for her books about family, a subject she knows well, as she has three children, a growing army of grandchildren, four cats and a dog named Amber.

Muriel and Ron live in an old Victorian home on a hill overlooking the Columbia River. Every day Muriel watches freighters, Coast Guard cutters, yachts and fishing boats come and go and speculates about the relationships of those aboard, and those they've left behind. She says it always inspires her.

Forrester Square
LEGACIES . LIES . LOVE .

MURIEL JENSEN
REINVENTING JULIA

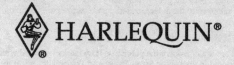

HARLEQUIN®

TORONTO • NEW YORK • LONDON
AMSTERDAM • PARIS • SYDNEY • HAMBURG
STOCKHOLM • ATHENS • TOKYO • MILAN • MADRID
PRAGUE • WARSAW • BUDAPEST • AUCKLAND

HARLEQUIN BOOKS
225 Duncan Mill Road, Don Mills,
Ontario, Canada M3B 3K9

ISBN 0-373-61268-0

REINVENTING JULIA

Muriel Jensen is acknowledged as the author of this work.

Copyright © 2003 by Harlequin Books S.A.

This edition published by arrangement with Harlequin Books S.A.

® and TM are trademarks of the publisher. Trademarks indicated with ® are registered in the United States Patent and Trademark Office, the Canadian Trade Marks Office and in other countries.

Visit us at www.eHarlequin.com

Printed in U.S.A.

Dear Reader,

As a young woman, I worked in the secretarial pool at the *Los Angeles Times* right downtown. Not only was the work exciting, but every lunch hour was an adventure in discovering the city. I've always thought there's really no such thing as a "big-city" man or woman, because big cities are all comprised of little neighborhoods where people can be as closely knit and involved in each other's lives as they are in a small town.

Helping populate Forrester Square reminded me of those days of crossing noisy traffic and weaving my way through the bustling crowds to discover a quiet little pocket of life flourishing in the middle of all that activity. People are people wherever they are. They care about each other and they cling together—particularly when many of them are part of a mysterious, life-altering past, and all of them are looking for love and a hopeful future.

Pull up a chair at Caffeine Hy's next door to the old three-story Italianate building on Sandringham Drive and become a part of our Belltown neighborhood. Look out the window. The action's about to begin.

Good wishes,

Muriel Jensen

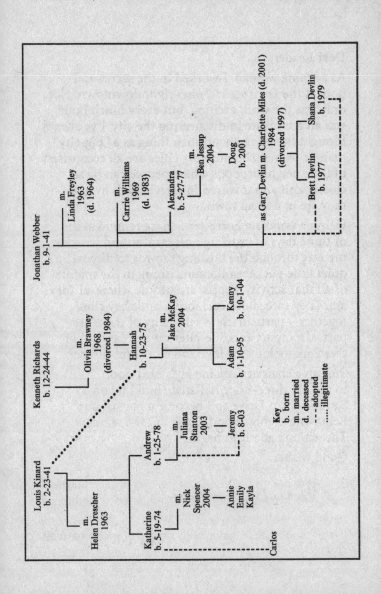

Kenneth Richards
b. 12-24-44

Louis Kinard
b. 2-23-41

m.
Helen Drescher
1963

m.
Olivia Brawney
1968
(divorced 1984)

Jonathan Webber
b. 9-1-41

m.
Linda Freyley
1963
(d. 1964)

m.
Carrie Williams
1969
(d. 1983)

as Gary Devlin m. Charlotte Miles (d. 2001)
1984
(divorced 1997)

Katherine
b. 5-19-74

Andrew
b. 1-25-78

Hannah
b. 10-23-75

Alexandra
b. 5-27-77

Shana Devlin
b. 1979

Brett Devlin
b. 1977

m.
Nick
Spencer
2004

m.
Juliana
Stanton
2003

m.
Jake McKay
2004

m.
Ben Jessup
2004

Annie
Emily
Kayla

Jeremy
b. 8-03

Adam
b. 1-10-95

Kenny
b. 10-1-04

Doug
b. 2001

Carlos

Key
b. born
m. married
d. deceased
- - - - adopted
· · · · · illegitimate

CHAPTER ONE

"I LIKED THE TALL BLONDE with the low-riding jeans and string of stars tattooed around her navel," Daniel Adler said lazily as he looked up at the darkening sky. "You think we'll make it home before it starts to rain?"

"You should have taken her up on that wink." Drew Kinard thought about walking faster, but he and Daniel were full of fried oysters and Shiraz, and it was just too much effort. Besides, if you ran from the rain in Seattle, you wouldn't stop until you were south of San Francisco. And the Belltown area of Seattle north of Pike Place Market was too interesting to rush through.

Once a featureless area of warehouses and low office buildings, Belltown had become the home of grunge musicians in the 1990s. A creative explosion brought writers and artists, followed by tourists and permanent residents looking for atmosphere and style. Belltown had gone upscale in the last decade and was now a hot neighborhood filled with busy boutiques and fancy restaurants.

"I'm sure she'd have been happy to go home with you," Drew needled his friend, "with a little encouragement."

Daniel's sigh was only moderately regretful. "Yeah, but women are a lot of trouble. And I'm a busy man."

Drew looked skeptical. "Right. You have time to put all that effort into clothes—Armani suits, Gucci shoes—just to look good in front of a judge while you're pleading a case, but you're too busy for women? Doesn't make sense to me."

Daniel laughed as a large raindrop plopped on his forehead. "It's to look good in front of the jury. And why didn't *you* return her wink?"

"Because it was aimed at you. And she wasn't my type."

"I thought you didn't have a type. There was that brainiac from Yale, and that perky do-gooder friend of Katherine's. Then there was the exotic dancer at…"

"Why are you keeping track of *my* love life?" Drew demanded good-naturedly. He and Daniel had been friends since they'd met at a networking session for young professionals three years ago. Harassment was an accepted part of their relationship. "Jealousy? Vicarious thrill?"

Daniel walked faster as that single drop developed into serious rain. "Simple fascination, I guess, that someone who looks like you can attract women."

"They don't all go for the buttoned-down type." Drew indicated his friend's immaculate attire with a sweep of his hand. Daniel's all-business attitude extended to more than just his appearance. Drew figured it had something to do with his childhood, but since Daniel seldom volunteered information about his past,

Drew never asked. "Some women prefer a more approachable man. One who looks…"

"Like a refugee from a dot-com company? Brains but no style?" Daniel pointed to Drew's more casual jeans, beige camp shirt, and thick dark hair, which always seemed a mess, no matter how often he combed it.

Drew pointed to a trash receptacle half a block away. "I'll bet I could slam-dunk you into that from here," he threatened.

Daniel laughed. "Then I'd have to sue you."

"That's all right. I have a good lawyer."

"I'm your lawyer."

"Oh, yeah."

Rain drummed heavily on the sidewalk and the windows of the old Italianate buildings that lined Sandringham Drive. When the wind suddenly picked up, the rain pelted down even harder, and the two men found themselves caught in a summer storm. They ran the half block to the Forrester Square Day Care building at 10, raced through the gate, then up the steps to the slight protection offered by the overhang of the doorway. Daniel's car was parked in front.

"The scuttlebutt," Daniel said, as he brushed water droplets off his suit, "is that you did a great job redesigning this building. One of my clients was talking about it at a Chamber meeting. He said you're the new name to watch in architecture in the city."

Drew was happy to hear that. He'd put everything he'd learned, and a lot of what seemed to be simple instinct, into the redesign of the old three-story sandstone that now housed his sister Katherine's day-care center. "I hope so," he said feelingly. "I like working on my own, but I need a really high-profile job to launch my company. I have dreams of one day having my own place where I no longer have to pay rent to my sister."

"Must be spooky to live above a day care," Daniel said seriously. "All those kids around all the time."

Drew shook his head. He had no problem with children. "The only bad part is having to be quiet if I'm home during the day. The babies and toddlers nap on the second floor, so I have to keep the music down. And, of course, I can't practice my clog dancing."

Daniel laughed. "You're an idiot." Then he sobered. "Hey, your dad's getting out pretty soon, isn't he."

Drew nodded. His chest constricted when he thought about it. Twenty years of a man's life wasted behind bars because of a crime he didn't commit.

"Yeah," he said, trying to sound unaffected. Though he had been only six years old when his father had gone to jail, Drew remembered how drastically his own life had changed. "Mom's excited. So's Katherine."

"And you?"

"It'll be great to have him back." His father had loved him, trusted him, treated him like another man. When Louis Kinard went to jail, Drew's mother and sister had become overprotective, trying hard to shield him from the whispers and accusing glances that came with his father's conviction. He'd balked against their cosseting and complained to his father about it one visiting day.

"You have to be the man of the family while I'm gone," his father had told him gravely in a private moment, "but sometimes that means letting your mother and sister fuss over you because it makes them feel better. Most important, Drew—you mustn't believe all the bad things you'll hear about me. I didn't do what they say I did, but I've been accused and convicted, and to most people, that's the same thing. Just remember how much I love you, and your mother and sister. The fact that I'm not with you doesn't change that one little bit."

He remembered the long drive home after that visit, and the realization that he'd felt braver than he had before.

Now, though, he was a man and not the child Louis Kinard had loved unconditionally. What would his dad think of Drew once he was able to spend much more time with him?

A loud slapping sound overhead snapped him out of his thoughts.

"He's going to think you're great," Daniel said, as though he'd seen right into Drew's mind. "And he'll probably continue to even after I try to set him straight. What the hell is that?"

Both stepped out into the rain to look up in the direction of the noise, which sounded a little like a loose sail.

Hanging down from the roof was a huge banner in the shape of a house, complete with smoking chimney, that had Forrester Square Day Care scrawled across it in a type that mimicked a child's handwriting. Attached to the banner and tied to a wrought-iron flower box on the third floor was a grand opening sign inviting everyone for a tour and refreshments on Saturday, August 30. One corner of the sign had slipped loose and slapped against the sandstone brick of the building. He could reach it, Drew thought, from his kitchen window.

"Want me to help you with that?" Daniel asked.

Drew shook his head. "No, thanks. I can do it. See you at the opening?"

"Wouldn't miss it. Katherine's one of my favorite clients. Thanks for dinner."

"Sure."

Daniel unlocked his car with the remote, hurried to it and drove off with a tap of his horn.

Once Drew was inside the building, the big double doors with their arched windows locked securely behind him. Though the opening ceremony wasn't scheduled until the 30th, the day care had been operating for two weeks now. At night when it closed, the quiet struck Drew like a sledgehammer. From 7:00 a.m., when children started arriving, until 5:30 p.m. and sometimes later, when they went home, the building was like a living thing, filled with shouts and laughter. But when the children were gone, it wasn't as though the building slept. It seemed to be ever alert, waiting.

Drew figured that was because the structure had been erected more than a century ago, and had had a fruitful life as a commercial building, then as a family residence. It didn't seem to like the idle times.

''Well, hell, *I'm* here,'' he told it as he went to the elevator and pushed the up button.

This elevator always seemed to become his personal time capsule, bringing alive memories of his past. When Drew was four or five, his father had worked short days at his office on Saturdays, and took Drew with him. The two would ride up the elevator together, then, armed with paper and pens, Drew would sit at an empty desk and doodle until his father was finished. Afterward they met his mother and sister for lunch downtown, where they'd been shopping.

In the old days, Louis Kinard, Jonathan Webber, and Kenneth Richards were partners in NorPac, a company that built commercial aircraft. But by the time Drew came along, the bottom had fallen out of the aircraft industry, and his father and his partners had turned NorPac into Eagle Aerotech, which created computer software for airplanes, with special applications for the military.

According to Drew's mother, Helen, the three friends had never regained the level of financial success they'd had in the beginning of their partnership, but life had still been very good.

Drew had the best toys and bikes, and the three families lived in the Queen Anne district around Forrester Square, for which Katherine's day care was named. Katherine spent most of her time with Jonathan's daughter, Alexandra, and Kenneth's daughter, Hannah, who was her partner in the day care. Drew had sometimes been welcome to join them if he left his water pistol behind. Those days had been idyllic.

Then one night a fire killed Jonathan and Carrie

Webber and left Alexandra to be raised by relatives in Montana. Drew's father was charged with embezzlement and the sale of sensitive military software on the black market, and sent to prison for twenty years.

Drew's perfect world had come to an abrupt halt.

The old memories seemed to be returning more often these days. Drew guessed that his father's impending homecoming prompted them.

Once the elevator reached his floor, he stepped out and unlocked the door to his apartment, then went straight down the long hallway that separated his large living room and kitchen from the two bedrooms and his office. He strode into the oak and yellow kitchen, climbed onto the counter and fought with the seldom-used window for a moment, then pushed it open. Drops of rain blew in at him as he prepared to battle the sign. He told himself he'd have to give Katherine a hard time about the lengths to which he was willing to go to be a supportive brother.

JULIA STANTON STUMBLED along in the rain, almost nine months pregnant, while equal parts of pain and terror threatened to paralyze her. She was somewhere in Belltown, a considerable distance from Pike Place Market, where she and Chloe Maddox had met to plan strategy and then discovered they'd been followed.

Her friend Chloe had insisted she be the decoy to allow Julia to escape in the opposite direction. But the stress of seeing Chloe pursued, compounded by her own trudge through Belltown's side streets in search of a cab or bus, had apparently precipitated labor.

It seemed she was going to deliver her baby now—in a deluge!

"Don't worry about me!" Chloe had ordered just before they'd separated. "I'm going to be fine." She'd patted Julia's swollen stomach. "Just keep my nephew safe and I'll get back to you with a solid case against your uncle in time to help you give birth."

Even the best-laid plans... Julia thought as rain soaked through her denim jumper, chilling her.

She glanced longingly at the coffee shop she'd just passed, closed for the night like the other businesses in the area, and felt any hope that she'd find help here sink to her toes. There wasn't a soul around.

She had a cell phone, but who would she call—911? An ambulance and police car would attract attention and create a paper trail wide enough to lead her uncle right to her.

Desperation made her groan aloud. "God, please," she prayed. "I can't give birth to this baby myself. I need an angel!"

She thought she heard an answer as another contraction tightened her abdomen and made her gasp. She found herself holding on to a wrought-iron fence in front of several steps that led up to a sandstone brick building. Panting as pain clutched her in a big fist, she dragged herself and her bag through the gate, intending to sit on the steps for a minute. But her legs suddenly gave way, and she desperately grabbed an iron railing to prevent herself from landing too hard.

Rain fell on her face as she sank backward onto the steps, one arm protectively over her stomach. She blinked against the pelting drops and thought she saw someone leaning out of the sky.

God? she wondered.

A little hysterical with pain, she decided the man she saw some distance above her wasn't leaning out of the sky, but an upstairs window.

"Hey!" a male voice shouted down at her. "Are you all right?"

She wanted to reply, but the cursed contraction went on and on, stealing her breath. Instead, she raised an arm toward him, hand outstretched in a "help me" gesture.

He disappeared.

She wanted to cry. And she might have indulged herself if she wasn't so determined that her baby would not be born on the sidewalk. She reached up for the railing to pull herself to a sitting position, but her body refused to budge.

"What happened?"

The man who'd been leaning out the window suddenly appeared beside her. He was tall and broad-shouldered, dressed in jeans and a beige shirt that was already soaked. As he leaned over her, she saw dark brown eyes assess her pregnant state, then swing to her face with an expression that was half frown, half smile.

"Forget that question," he said, kneeling on the stair beside her. "The baby's coming?"

"Yes," she replied on a gasp. "Quickly."

"Can you stand?"

"I don't think so."

"Okay. Put your arm around my neck."

"You can't lift me," she said, even as she did as he asked. "We're too heavy!"

"Well." He slipped an arm under her back and one rather intimately under her hips. "Let's see if my membership at the gym has been worth the money. Ready?"

"I don't think you should…" she began, certain they'd be lying here side by side in a minute, she delivering a baby and he paralyzed with back strain.

But miraculously she was off the steps and in his arms and he was striding into the building.

"I'll take you up to my apartment," he said, going to an elevator at the back of a long hallway. "I'll call 911, then we'll call your husband."

"No," she said, trying to keep the panic out of her voice as she held tightly to him. The elevator door opened and he stepped inside. "We can't call anybody. Please."

He studied her suspiciously. "What do you mean? We have to call for help. You're about to have a baby."

"Yes," she said with a serious look into his eyes. He was drenched and so was she, and they left a small puddle in the middle of the elevator as he stepped out into the third-floor hallway, still carrying her. "I know what to do. The book's in my bag."

"The book?"

"On delivering your own baby."

"Yeah, right." He walked through a doorway and down another hallway, then into a room that was cool and filled with shadows. Carefully he lowered her onto a soft mattress. "I'll put you at the end of the bed until we can get you into dry clothes."

Before he disappeared he flipped a light on and she stared up at white ceilings with crown molding, cream-colored walls covered with architectural drawings and forest-green draperies.

Quickly he reappeared with several fluffy white towels. He lifted her head gently and spread a towel out beneath her, then handed her a second one.

"Is there something in that bag you can put on?" he asked.

"A nightgown," she replied, then groaned as another contraction took hold of her.

He turned from her bag and headed to the bedside table, where there was a phone.

"No, please!" she begged, her teeth gritted as another wave of pain gripped her. If her uncle discovered where she was, it would be all over for her and her baby. "Please don't call!"

He hesitated for an instant, then came back to her. She caught his hand to hold him there.

"Look," he said urgently, "I'm not a cop or a cabdriver. I don't have experience delivering babies. And I'm sure no latent talent is going to magically surface and allow me to help you, so please! Let me call 911."

She clutched his hand as the pain crested, seized her for what felt like an eternity, then began to recede. She had to make him understand.

She had to lie.

"My...husband is abusive and part of a mob family," she fabricated, recalling the plot of a TV movie she'd just seen. "He wants to groom this baby to take over for him just as he's done for his father. If his family finds out where I am, they'll make me come back. Or worse, they'll let me go but keep the baby. Please."

She couldn't tell if he believed her or not, and for one horrible moment, she thought her made-up story sounded worse than her real one.

"What's your name?" he asked finally.

She had to lie again; everyone knew the Stanton name. Her uncle was a United States senator, for heaven's sake. Remembering that the bag she carried was initialed, she answered, "Jeanie Shaw."

"Shaw doesn't sound like a mob name."

"Jeannie Shaw Abruzzo," she amended. "Marco Abruzzo was a big mistake, so I'm reclaiming my maiden name." He still watched her suspiciously, and in an attempt to distract him, she asked, "Who are you? And what are you doing all alone in this empty building?"

"I'm Drew Kinard." He didn't look distracted, just willing to humor her. "My sister owns this building and has a day care on the first and second floor. I'll get your nightgown."

DREW DUG past a sweatshirt and a small purse and found a voluminous yellow cottony thing. He held it up to ask her if that was it, but she was in the throes of another contraction so he tossed it on the bed and took her hand again. She ground it in hers, breathing heavily.

He'd wager her story was a crock. After a family

dinner several months ago, he'd been forced to sit with his mother and sister and watch a movie on the Women's Channel that had exactly the same plot. But whoever Jeanie Shaw Abruzzo really was, she was about to deliver a baby and—God save him—he was going to have to help her.

The moment the contraction passed, he got her out of the cumbersome jumper and the simple white blouse underneath. He dried off her shoulders and her arms, wondering what to do about the wet slip clinging to her breasts and her bulbous belly.

"Can you manage the rest," he asked, "or do you need help?"

She nodded, running the towel over her face. "I can do it."

"While you're doing that," he said, going for a no-nonsense approach to thwart her resistance, "I'm going to call a doctor friend of mine…" She opened her mouth to protest, but he kept talking. "He won't tell a soul, I promise. But he's nearby. He's not an obstetrician, but he's the head of pediatrics at Seattle Memorial. I'm sure he can help us. All right?"

Her pain-filled blue eyes studied him worriedly. "You're sure he won't tell anyone?"

"I'm sure."

"I don't like it."

"I know."

"If you're wrong about him," she said gravely, "and anything happens, I'm coming after you."

She was average in height, and he guessed that without the pregnancy, she probably weighed all of 110 pounds. But he took her at her word. Her face was pale, and strands of damp blond hair clung to her cheeks, but her expression was fiercely determined. "I understand. You get out of that slip, and I'll get Ben."

Ben Jessup, head of pediatrics at Seattle Memorial Hospital, was on the Kiwanis fund-raising committee with Drew and Daniel, and worked out at the same gym.

"Why don't you bring her to the hospital?" Ben asked when Drew explained his problem.

"She claims to be on the run from an abusive husband," Drew said quickly. "I'm not sure I swallow that, but she's got some kind of problem to be all alone and in labor on my doorstep. Ben, I'm dying here. I don't know what to do for her. Can you come?"

"Yeah, I can come. I've finished my shift, but if there's a problem, she should be here where we're equipped..."

"She won't even consider it. Please, Ben. If I'm alone with her when this baby comes, I'm going to do awful things to you."

He heard the smile in Ben's voice. "Then I'll be right there."

Drew ran back into the bedroom, where she was puffing like a locomotive, the coverlet clutched in her hands. Another contraction. He didn't want to think about how close they were.

She'd managed to change into the nightgown, but her small feet stuck out from under it, still clad in sandals.

He went to put one knee beside her on the bed and

leaned over her. "He's coming," he said, taking a corner of the towel under her head and dabbing at the perspiration on her forehead and cheeks. "Hang on, help's on the way."

"Tell Jeremy to hang on," she said breathlessly. "He's the one who's in such a hurry."

Jeremy, he concluded, was the baby.

"You're sure it's a boy?" He pulled off her sandals.

She nodded. "Ultrasound in my…my fifth month."

"I know you don't want your…husband to know, but what about your parents?"

She studied him, wondering, probably, if his brief hesitation suggested he doubted her story. He tried to wipe all suspicion from his expression. She had enough to deal with at the moment.

"Gone," she said simply.

"Siblings?"

"None."

"What about a friend?"

She looked at him with an expression that was at once touching and sad. "You're it, Drew Kinard."

Drew sympathized with her loneliness, not because he understood it, but because he'd *never* known it and couldn't imagine having to live with it. Though his father had been in prison most of Drew's life, Louis Kinard had wanted to know everything that went on with his family, and Drew's mother had kept him as involved in their lives as she could through letters, photos and visits.

And with his mother and sister coddling him at

every turn, Drew never had a chance to be lonely. Sometimes it was a challenge just to find time to be alone.

He plumped the pillows at the head of the bed, threw the coverlet back, then drew Jeanie up against them. She made a small sound of approval. "That feels good," she said.

He tossed her wet clothes into a corner and pulled the dry sheet up over her.

When the doorbell rang, he hurried to answer it. It was all he could do not to wrap his arms around Ben, who was still in his hospital coat. Drew pulled him inside.

"Her name's Jeanie Shaw," he said, leading him into the bedroom.

"I'm Ben, Jeanie," Ben said as he offered his hand. "How're you doing?"

"I wish I was shopping," she replied breathlessly, reaching up to shake his hand. "I hope I didn't spoil your Sunday night plans."

"Nah." Ben put his bag on the chair beside the bed and removed a stethoscope. "I was just about to leave the hospital anyway."

"To go home and relax," she guessed apologetically.

"Nope." He drew the blanket down to her knees and put the stethoscope to her stomach. "I have a son who's two and a half. I don't relax much. I told my weekend sitter I might be a while."

She smiled. "The baby seems to have taken a violent dislike to his accommodations. Ah!"

Another contraction overtook her, and Drew, unwilling to watch her suffer further now that Ben was here, took off for the kitchen. He made a pot of coffee, thinking Ben might want some when he was finished. Then he paced the living room, watching the rain beat against the Palladian windows, the lights of Seattle distorted through the raindrops.

As minutes ticked away, he felt the atmosphere tighten, the pace quicken. Sounds from the bedroom had turned from simple conversation to calmly spoken instructions interspersed with Jeanie's occasional cries of distress. Drew was torn between a desire to leave the apartment and escape the sound, or burst into the bedroom and demand that Ben relieve her misery.

Then Ben shouted his name.

"Yeah?" He went to the head of the hallway and saw his friend leaning out of the bedroom doorway. Ben had removed the hospital coat and his tie, and rolled up his sleeves.

"I could use you in here," he said.

Drew went despite an urgent impulse to run in the other direction.

Jeanie was pale and exhausted and gulping in air.

Ben pointed him to the head of the bed. "I want you to sit behind her and support her back," he said. "This baby's coming on the next push. Hold the pillow against you for her to lean on—that's it. Wrap your arms around her and hold on."

Easier said than done, Drew quickly realized. Except for the large mound of the baby, there was nothing to hold on to. But that problem was solved for him when Jeanie, apparently pleased to have something to grasp, pulled his arms down under her breasts and held them there, clearly readying herself for the last push.

"I'm sorry I did this to you," she said, leaning against him with all her weight. Her voice sounded weak, as though she didn't have an ounce of energy left.

"No need to apologize," he assured her. "All I had planned for the evening was a Mariners game on television."

"Okay, Jeanie," Ben said, sitting on the bed and positioned to receive the baby, "this time I want you to give it all you've got."

She struggled to marshal what little force she had left. "Okay," she said wearily.

"Dig in your heels and push. Right now! Push!"

Drew sensed the energy mount in her, heard her cry build, then felt all ten of her fingernails rip into the flesh on the backs of his hands. He bore the small pain quietly, imagining what she was going through.

"We've got a head with lots of fuzzy blond hair!" Ben said jubilantly as Jeanie groaned and gasped. "Take a breath and give me one more push!"

She did.

Drew held tightly as she pushed backward against him, screaming mightily.

"A shoulder!" he shouted. "Another shoulder! Yes! He's here! All of him!"

"Is he okay?" she demanded urgently, straining to see.

"Perfect," Ben replied, working with the cord. Then he held the baby up, a very red but apparently perfect, squalling little bundle of attitude, clearly upset with his change of residence.

After clearing his eyes and nose and severing the cord, Ben placed him in Jeanie's arms. She wept noisily, then raised her free arm and put her hand to Drew's face. She leaned back against his shoulder to look up at him.

"Thank you," she whispered.

"Happy to be of service," he replied. He felt completely humbled by the miracle he'd just helped bring about.

Then it occurred to him that he was going to have to play host to Jeanie and Jeremy Shaw for a couple of days. The baby was scarily tiny, and his mother was in no condition to go anywhere. Her story was flimsy, but something had driven her out into a rainstorm, about to deliver a baby. He intended to help her evade whatever or whoever it was she feared until she and the baby were strong enough to move on.

CHAPTER TWO

IT AMAZED JULIA that a woman could be filled with joy and awash in grief at the same time. But that was how her stunningly beautiful and wrinkly little son made her feel as he lay in her arms.

His tiny body was perfect, the very fact that he'd been born safe and well such a miracle under the circumstances that she felt unutterably grateful. Yet it broke her heart that his father had died before even knowing he was going to have a son, and that Jeremy would never know the good, kind, dedicated man Devon Maddox had been.

She forced the grief aside and decided to think positively. Despite the losses in her life, she had her baby.

Ben gave her a few basic instructions in nursing while Drew went downstairs to bring up a Moses basket, diapers, and a few other things from the day-care center. Luckily for her his sister ran the center and had entrusted Drew with a master key.

While Julia watched her son begin to suckle greedily, Ben changed the bedding. "The nurses always make this look so easy," he said as he encouraged her to slide over to the fresh side of the sheets while he finished making the bed. "There. Comfortable?"

She winced. "Not precisely, no. But relieved and very, very grateful to you for coming to help."

"Drew told me about your...*husband,*" he said with a frowning glance at her. He hesitated over the word, just as Drew had done, and she wondered if she detected irony in his tone. "I hope you'll be reporting his harassment to the police."

"I will." She did her best to sound convincing. "As soon as I'm feeling steady on my feet."

"Good. Because this little guy deserves to be safe."

She smoothed the baby's tufty hair. "Yes, I know."

"And so does Drew," Ben said. "He's had a few tough breaks himself, but he's always the first to lend a helping hand. I'd hate to think something might happen to him for sheltering you." Whether or not he believed her story, he seemed to be convinced she was trouble either way.

Her brief half hour of tranquility dissolved in the realization that she posed a threat to her Good Samaritan if her uncle did find her. She'd taken every precaution, but Randolph Stanton was a desperate man. She was convinced he had killed her fiancé, and now he was after her.

"I'll be gone in the morning," she said.

The doctor straightened to study her gravely. "That's not what I mean, Jeanie. You're not going to help your baby or Drew by endangering yourself. Just...think things through."

She nodded dutifully.

He had no way of knowing she'd already done that,

and no matter how things looked, she'd been running to safety and not away from responsibility when she'd found herself on Drew's doorstep.

Drew returned with an armload of baby provisions, and Julia focused her attention on the here and now. The doctor helped her ease into one of Drew's T-shirts, the only available alternative to another nightgown. He helped her diaper the baby and told her what to watch for in the way of behavior.

The baby was now asleep, and Ben put him in the basket and placed it in the upholstered chair, which he moved closer to the bed.

"You have to rest," he advised, "because he'll be up every few hours to nurse and you're going to have an exhausting week or so. Maybe more if he doesn't settle into a routine. You need to eat well, remembering that the baby's getting all his nourishment from you."

"Okay."

"Drink milk, water, eat protein three times a day. The occasional dessert's okay, but go easy on the empty calories. You're still eating for two."

She nodded.

"I think you're both going to be fine, but Drew knows how to reach me if you have any problems. Don't hesitate to call."

Then Drew was walking him to the door.

Her optimism wavered as the reality of her situation struck. She'd just had a baby, her uncle had had her fiancé killed and was now probably looking for her, and she had no place to go.

Of course she did, she told herself bracingly, desperate to fight off the mood. She'd go to a hotel just as she and Chloe had planned. Nothing was different. A nice man had helped her out so she could deliver her baby safely, but he owed her no more than that and she certainly didn't expect anything else.

The feeling of security had been nice, but now she had to cope on her own. And she could; she always had.

She just wished she didn't have to.

DREW RETURNED to the bedroom, surprised to find Jeanie with tears in her eyes. She'd endured labor and childbirth so heroically that it worried him to see her in tears. He knelt beside the bed so that he could look into the dangerously uncertain expression on her face. What was behind the lie? he wondered. What was her secret? Something dark, he guessed, from the near-despair in her eyes. He found himself wishing he could help, but she'd placed him on the other side of that lie, and it reduced his options.

Her blond hair, drying now after being drenched in perspiration, was a wild halo around her. He suppressed an unexpected impulse to touch it.

"Are you in pain?" he asked. Stupid question. How could she not be?

"No," she said, her voice choked.

"Worried about your...husband?"

She looked at him, studied his eyes. "Not at the moment," she replied finally.

"The baby?"

"Yeah." She tightened her lips, her expression mournful. "It's just occurred to me that I know how to hold him, and feed him and that's about it. What have I done?''

He rubbed her shoulder gently. ''Well, according to Ben, that's all Jeremy's going to need for a while, so you're better equipped than you think.''

''Yeah,'' she said skeptically.

He fluffed her pillow and urged her to lie down, pulling the blanket up over her shoulder. ''Ben also said that your moods will be erratic for a few days because your hormones are all over the place. That's probably all this is. Try to get some sleep and you'll feel better when you wake up.''

She tipped her head back slightly on the pillow to look into his eyes. ''You were probably a very happy bachelor with nothing to worry about but how the Mariners are doing and where to take your next date.''

He smiled. ''Well, you're right about the Mariners, anyway. But I'm off women for a while. I haven't had a date since Suzie Carneiro told me she thought I was dull.''

''You're kidding!''

''Well, she said architecture was dull. Same thing.''

''She's ridiculous.''

''That's what I thought. Go to sleep. I'll fix you something to eat when you wake up.''

''I can find something to eat if you have places to go.''

''Nope. No place to go.''

''No people to see?''

''Nope. Did that before you arrived.''

She sighed wearily and closed her eyes. "Eggs sound really good."

"Okay. Coming up the moment you wake up."

"Thank you," she said, her voice drifting.

"Sure."

He checked the basket. The baby slept on his back, looking very normal, if a little red. He watched for the subtle rise and fall of the soft blanket that covered him, a blanket Jeanie had had packed in her bag. Once he'd confirmed the baby was breathing, he flipped off the light and left the room, leaving the door slightly ajar.

"God," he thought with less anxiety than surprise as he headed for the kitchen. "What a day!"

BEN CERTAINLY KNEW his stuff. Jeremy was up at 2:00, just before 4:00, and shortly after 6:00. Jeanie ate small amounts of egg the first time he woke up, a piece of toast the second time, but after the third, she pleaded for a cup of coffee—decaf, at least.

"You're going to have to get some sleep," she said, once she'd tucked Jeremy back in his basket. She sat propped against her pillows, and Drew perched at the foot of the bed. "You've been up with me every single time."

"I'm just being a good support staff," he said, offering her a cookie from a bag of chocolate-covered Oreos he kept on hand.

Her eyes widened and she snatched one hungrily. "They're hardly nutritious, but I *love* these."

"Me, too. We're lucky there are any left, though.

My sister's foster son, Carlos, stayed the night with me a few days ago while Katherine was out of town.''

"How old is he?''

"He's twelve. Big on Nintendo, skateboards, Christina Aguilera and chocolate-covered Oreos.''

"Sounds like a pretty normal boy.''

He nodded. "He is now that Katherine's taken him in. The court removed him from his druggie parents when he was seven.''

"Lucky boy.''

She was staring at something beyond him, her eyes unfocused. Then she seemed to notice his unspoken question and took another sip of her coffee. "My parents died when I was eleven,'' she said. "A train crash. My father was president of an athletic supplies company and hated to fly, so they took the train everywhere. Wasn't as safe as he thought.'' She played with the spoon he'd given her, though she hadn't put anything into her coffee. "They were great. My dad was big and gruff with a marshmallow heart, and my mother was smart and organized but lots of fun. I still miss them something awful.'' She took another quick sip of her coffee, as though she needed it. "Now, particularly. I hate to think Jeremy won't know them.''

"You'll have to tell him all about them,'' he said, realizing it was feeble comfort. His father had been gone a long time, but at least he was alive. He could only imagine what her loss felt like.

"Can I have another Oreo?'' she asked.

He handed her the bag.

"Do you have to go to work this morning?" she asked.

He shook his head and hooked a thumb in the direction of his office at the end of the hall. "I work from home, though when the project's in construction, I do spend a lot of time on the site."

"How did you get interested in architecture?"

"Built my own tree house," he said, smiling as he remembered the project. "It was very cool. Probably the only tree house around with flying buttresses."

She blinked. "What are those, anyway?"

"You see them in cathedrals. Large archlike things sticking out the sides that resist outward pressure. They're functional but also beautifully decorative. Of course, mine were a little less impressive, but I connected them to the next tree. It looked like a clan of Ewoks lived there when I was finished."

She giggled. The baby stirred in his little basket, already reacting to the sound of her voice. Something about that softened a hard place in Drew's heart.

"How old were you?"

"Eight, I think. As I recall, I took apart a ladder, a doghouse, and an old desk to get the lumber."

"Wasn't the dog unhappy?"

"No. He slept in my room anyway."

"And your parents weren't mad about the ladder and the desk?"

He opened his mouth to tell her about his father, then thought better of it. She'd just had a very difficult day. She didn't need his personal issues added to her own.

"No," he replied.

She waited as though wanting more, but when it wasn't forthcoming, she handed him back the cup. "Thank you for the coffee."

He stood, their two empty cups hooked in one finger. "I guess you're ready to go back to sleep."

"Nothing like having a baby and being awakened every two hours to fight insomnia."

"Good night," he said, though dawn was visible through the thin slit between the draperies. Then he grinned as he remembered Jeremy's two-hour schedule. "Or, rather, see you at eight."

Not if I have anything to say about it, Julia vowed silently as she snuggled into her pillow.

DESPITE HER EXHAUSTION, sleep eluded Julia as it had since her fiancé, Devon, had gone missing in February. Her mind insisted on going over the incredible events of the last two days as though repetition would make sense of them.

As an investigative reporter for the *Seattle Post-Intelligencer,* Devon had gotten close to many unsavory cases in his career, and his colleagues had suspected his disappearance suggested he'd finally gotten *too* close.

Devon and his sister, Chloe, had grown up in a small newspaper office run by their parents in eastern Oregon. Both had the journalist's zeal for truth and justice, though Chloe had taken a year off to try her hand at writing fiction while Devon stuck to hard news.

When Devon disappeared back in February, Julia and Chloe had searched his apartment, and his editor

had checked the files on his computer at the office.
But they'd found nothing that pointed directly to foul
play.

Then the police officer who'd been investigating
Devon as a missing person had called Saturday to tell
her they were raising his car out of the Sound. It
looked as though he'd fallen asleep at the wheel and
driven off one of the area's many bridges.

Neither Julia nor Chloe could believe that. On Sunday they'd gone together to his Beacon Hill apartment
to clean it out after the landlord insisted he wanted to
attract a new renter before the publicity of Devon's
death made him unable to.

Going through Devon's things the day after his
body was discovered had been grisly, but when Chloe
discovered a disk hidden in a boot box at the back of
his closet, it had validated their suspicions that his
death was not an accident.

Chloe had fed the disk into Devon's laptop. It contained only one file entitled SENRAN, and on it was
a list of what appeared to be purchases and expenses.
In a column at the side was a note indicating how
each item had been masked on an expense account to
appear legitimate. Included were articles of clothing,
plane tickets, restaurant meals, miscellaneous items.
Everything had been categorized as a business expense, including something cryptically identified as
IT, which had cost a monthly $20,000.

A list of projects followed, and after each was a
dollar amount that had turned up missing at the project's completion.

Julia reread the list and exclaimed under her breath,

"Oh, my God!" These were projects overseen by her uncle as chairman of the Washington Improvements Committee. "It's my uncle!"

"What?" Chloe studied the screen then gasped in a hushed voice, "Of course! SENRAN. Senator Randolph!"

Julia had tried to think clearly. Devon had probably died for this.

For some time now she'd been subsidizing her uncle to the tune of $20,000 a month, money he claimed he needed for repayment of campaign expenses. Julia had doubted that was the real reason because she'd personally covered most of his expenses, but he was notorious for living beyond his means. And she'd been working with a lobbying group by then and had other things on her mind. "Is that everything on the file?" she asked Chloe.

Chloe scrolled down and discovered what looked like random notes.

Where is Alyssa Crawford? was underlined.

"Who," Chloe had asked, "is Alyssa Crawford?"

"My uncle's intern," Julia replied. "She took a job at the embassy in Turkey, last I heard."

Chloe read aloud several notes that followed. "Never arrived in Ankara. Seattle apartment still furnished, gym membership active, deli charge account still open. Maxie says SENRAN and Alyssa went to Giorgio's once before Christmas, once after."

That was followed by the dates, "Feb. 9—12."

"That was our trip to New York for your birthday!" Julia whispered to Chloe. Her fingertip followed the next note on the screen. "SENRAN in Barbados 11-15.'' Devon had disappeared on February 11th.

''He was checking something out at your house, while we were gone and your uncle was in Barbados,'' Chloe said, reading her brother's last note. ''Must have been something he didn't want you interfering with.''

''But…what?''

Julia had stared at the screen, unable to believe the implications. Her uncle had come to live with her when her parents died, assuming control of her monthly allowance in accordance with her father's will.

He'd never been warm—in fact he'd seldom been around. It was clear from the beginning that he'd stayed because of the provisions of the will, his proximity to her money and her willingness to share it when she'd turned twenty-one and could control it herself. Though she didn't come into her full inheritance until she turned twenty-five, her wealth was still impressive. He'd never showed any real feeling for her, but did that make him capable of murder?

Blackmail? Devon had written. Followed by *Would explain the $20,000.*

Chloe's eyes widened with sudden understanding. ''I'll bet the intern learned about these phony expenditures, blackmailed him, and he offed her. And Devon found proof.'' She pushed the button on the printer and pages began whooshing out. ''We're taking this to the police.''

''I can't believe Devon didn't tell me about any of it,'' Julia said, scrolling down still farther.

"I imagine he didn't want to accuse your uncle and upset you until he could prove everything."

"Oh, oh," Julia said.

"What?" Chloe leaned over her shoulder.

Julia directed Chloe's attention to one final note. *Suspect Harwood's involvement.*

"Who's Harwood?" Chloe asked.

"The police commissioner," Julia replied, feeling trapped and mildly panicky. Harwood had helped her uncle plan a law-and-order platform and had spent many evenings at her home.

"You have to move out of the house and into a hotel," Chloe said with sudden resolve, "while I finish what Devon started."

"What?" Julia had demanded. "You can't..."

"Yes, I can." Chloe had squared up the printed pages, folded them in half and put them in her purse. "You're not going anywhere unnoticed with that belly, so I'm going to find this Maxie person and figure out what he and Devon talked about, then I'm going to try to find Alyssa Crawford. Either she disappeared for her own safety, or—" her voice lowered an octave "—she's dead."

Dead. Dead like Devon. The two friends had held out hope over the long six months that Devon would be found alive, but now Julia saw her own raw grief reflected in Chloe's eyes. She wrapped her arms around her friend and they held each other for a long moment.

"Now," Chloe said briskly, "all we can do is keep Devon's baby safe and make sure he didn't die for nothing."

Julia nodded. "I'll go home and pack a bag."

"No. You shouldn't go back there."

"It's all right. My uncle's at the capital this week."

But he wasn't. When Julia got home, she found him wandering the large living room with a Scotch in his hand.

Randolph Stanton was tall and distinguished-looking, with gray hair and a gigolo's taste for clothes. In his younger days he'd reminded her of her father, but without his sense of humor and ability to find pleasure in everyday life. He could feign affability in public for his constituents, but despite his intelligence and his gift for politics, there was a brooding quality to his nature that had always held her at a distance, even when she'd helped run his campaign.

Julia had struggled to keep all she'd learned that day out of her eyes.

Her uncle put an arm around her shoulders and walked her to the winding staircase. "I'm sorry about Devon," he said. "I came home as soon as I heard."

She smiled politely.

"I understand you closed up his apartment today," he said, jiggling his glass so that the ice tinkled. The unspoken question, "And what did you find?" lingered ominously between them.

It was on the tip of her tongue to ask him how he knew where she'd been, but she decided against it.

"A charity's picking up his furniture," she said instead.

"I've booked two tickets to Barbados," he said, smiling. "You need to get away. I'll take you to my place there and you can just relax for a couple of weeks. Sit in the sun. Catch up on your reading. We can celebrate your birthday there.''

Her twenty-fifth birthday. Fear strummed a cold finger down her spine.

She wanted to slap his hands away, to run far and fast, but she made herself reply calmly, ''Thank you, but I still have a lot to do. And the airlines won't let me fly in the last month of pregnancy.''

''I've chartered a flight for us.'' He glanced at his watch. ''I'm sure that's a precaution just for women with at-risk pregnancies. Go get packed. It'll do you good.''

She'd pretended to comply and walked up the stairs, her heart hammering in her breast. Once in her room, she'd locked herself in the bathroom, then called Chloe and told her to meet her at the end of the driveway.

''How are you going to get out of there?'' Chloe had asked, her voice tight with concern.

''I'm supposed to be packing,'' she whispered. ''If he sees me go downstairs, I'll pretend I'm taking my bag to the car. Then I'll drive away. Be there, Chloe!''

''I'm on my way.''

And the plan had worked. She'd reached the car unnoticed, driven to the end of the lane and quickly transferred to Chloe's car. It wasn't until they tried to lose themselves in the crowd at Pike Place Market that she realized they'd been followed by her uncle's assistant and his driver. Both men had given her the creeps ever since he'd hired them at the first of the year, and she'd been grateful that they spent most of the time with him at the capital.

After ditching Chloe's car, Julia and Chloe made their way to an ATM so Julia could withdraw cash. Huddled behind a display of bank brochures, they'd made their hasty plans, then Chloe had made a run for it to allow Julia to escape.

Now, here she was in Drew Kinard's apartment, safe and sound—at least for the moment.

But she knew her uncle was ruthless. He'd waged a rough campaign and summarily fired anyone who disagreed with his decisions. He'd tolerated her insistence that going to the press with the sexual escapades of his opponent's young daughter was off-limits only because she'd paid for so much of his campaign.

Julia wondered what would have happened to her if she'd accompanied him to Barbados. With her gone, he was next in line for her inheritance.

She shuddered and closed her eyes against the images.

CHAPTER THREE

JULIA SLEPT FITFULLY for an hour, then woke up just before seven. Everything was still quiet. Ignoring her discomfort, she carefully slipped on the pale blue sweatsuit she'd packed. She moved gingerly as she collected some of the supplies Drew had brought up for her, then pulled a bill out of the small purse in the front pocket of her bag and left it on the dresser.

Jeremy was fast asleep in his basket. Praying that he would remain asleep until she gained the sidewalk, she scooped up the basket silently and pulled the door open. Every muscle in her body protested her own weight, much less that of the baby and her bag. But she had to get out of here. Her presence was dangerous to Drew.

She stepped stealthily out into the hall, waited a moment to make sure there was no other sound, then tiptoed past a closed door. Probably where Drew was working. Once she made it through the apartment door to the elevator, she was sure she was home free.

Until the elevator door opened and she saw Drew standing there with a bag of groceries. Her heart sank. The last thing she wanted at this point was a confrontation.

He stepped off the elevator with a dark frown,

caught her arm and held her in place when she would have stepped on.

"Where are you going?" he asked.

"I...have an appointment," she said, schooling her expression to appear imperious and determined.

He didn't seem to notice. "You had a baby nine hours ago. That wouldn't be smart."

"I was there, remember?" she said quietly, tugging at the arm he held. "You'll notice I *have* the baby, and smart or not, I'm going. Thank you for all you've done."

He held on to her. "You're very pale."

"I'm blond. I'm supposed to be pale."

"*Why* are you leaving?"

"I told you."

"I don't believe you have an appointment."

"That's your choice. Now, if you don't let me go, I'll scream bloody murder."

"But that would attract the police, or someone who'd undoubtedly want to call them," he pointed out smoothly, "and I'm sure you wouldn't want that."

Though she appreciated his concern, she was losing her patience with him. "I want to go," she said with forced calmness, "because it's a free country, and I should be able to do what I want to do."

"Now that you have a baby," he replied in the same tone, "it's still a free country, but you're obliged to think of what's best for him before considering what you want. That's what my mother always did. Still does, in fact, even though Katherine and I are well over twenty-one."

"The baby," she said stubbornly, "wants to go, too."

The elevator door closed. Julia looked at it in exasperation.

"Then you should explain to Jeremy that Dr. Jessup said he shouldn't be moved for a couple of days."

She studied him doubtfully. "He never said that."

"He did."

"Not to me."

"You didn't walk him to the door and get all the last-minute instructions."

Julia didn't know whether to believe him or not.

WHILE JEANIE STOOD there, looking undecided, Drew took the basket from her and headed into the apartment. He couldn't just let her walk away and leave her and the baby to the vagaries of fate.

She dropped her bag just inside the door and followed him into the kitchen, threatening his back.

"Look, don't think because you helped me out last night that I—"

"We'll talk about it over breakfast," he said, placing the basket in the middle of the counter. The wrinkled infant was fast asleep.

"I don't *have* to talk about it with you," she said, grabbing the handle of the basket. "I appreciate all you've—"

"You're going to wake him," he interrupted.

She stopped in exasperation.

He reached into the grocery bag and held up a fresh orange. "Ever had French toast seasoned with orange zest? Saw Emeril do it—it's wonderful."

"I don't want…oh!"

Drew turned at the surprised sound in her voice and saw his sister, Katherine, standing in the kitchen doorway. In a long, loose yellow dress patterned with small flowers, she looked very much like someone who worked with children. Niceness was written all over her from her gentle brown eyes to her wide, warm smile.

But a subtle change took place in her manner the moment her glance fell on Jeanie, then went to the baby in the basket. She tossed her shoulder-length brown hair, and it was as though that action flipped a switch. Instead of the lovely woman who was everyone's friend, she was now the protective big sister who watched his every move and felt she had the right to comment on it.

"Good morning," she said a little stiffly. She carried a bakery box and a clipboard.

"Hey, sis," he greeted her, putting the orange down. "You're just in time for French toast."

"I thought we had a meeting this morning," she said, waggling the clipboard. "To talk about the grand opening."

He wasn't surprised that he'd completely forgotten.

"That's right." He beckoned her into the room. "Slipped my mind."

"Did it also slip your mind that it's less than two weeks away?"

"Of course not. I apologize. We can get to it right after breakfast. First, though, I'd like you to meet Jeanie Shaw. Jeanie, this is my sister, Katherine."

Though Katherine remained in the doorway, Jeanie

stepped toward her and offered her hand. "Hi, Katherine," she said with a graciousness that had been lacking in their conversation of a moment ago. "Come on in and have your meeting. I was just leaving."

Drew put his hand on the basket when she would have taken it.

"Jeanie, don't be stubborn," he said quietly. "It isn't safe for you to go. Sit down, we'll have breakfast, and we can talk about what you..."

"What do you mean, it isn't safe?" Katherine asked. She never considered his business private. "Why not?"

"She's on the run from an abusive husband," Drew explained, though Jeanie's eyes pleaded with him to be quiet and let her go. "And she just had Jeremy yesterday."

Katherine frowned and went toward the basket. "This is Jeremy?" The frown instantly became a soft smile as she put her things down on the counter and reached an index finger into the basket to stroke a tiny hand. Then she looked up in puzzlement. "I don't understand. He was born yesterday?"

Jeanie retreated to a padded kitchen chair and sat gingerly on it, her expression dismal.

"Last night," Drew replied. "About ten o'clock."

"Six minutes after ten," Jeanie corrected without looking at them.

"And she's already out of the hospital?"

Drew expelled a breath. "Jeanie didn't have him in the hospital. She had him here."

"What?" Katherine gasped. "You delivered a baby?"

"Actually, Ben Jessup delivered Jeremy. Here."

Drew picked up the basket from the counter, put it in Katherine's arms, then pointed her to the table. "Jeanie will tell you all about it while I make breakfast."

Jeanie looked daggers at him, but she did relate the story of their eventful evening. She described her escape from her husband when their taxicab was involved in an accident, and then Drew's discovery of her collapsed on the front steps.

He glanced up from flipping French toast. "I was trying to fix the grand opening banner, which had gotten loose in the storm." He pointed the turner at Katherine. "It's all your fault. I was doing you a favor."

She made a face at him and turned her attention to Jeanie. "Did you report your husband to the police?"

Jeanie shook her head. "He's part of a crime family. Even if they did pick him up, he'd be home again before the paperwork was finished."

Katherine sat back in her chair and raised an eyebrow at her. "A crime family? You mean...the Mafia?"

"Yes," Jeanie said. "He wants the baby. His family consider themselves some kind of royal line. I just want to get far away from him."

"Ben told me she and the baby should rest for a few days," Drew said to Katherine as he delivered two plates of golden brown French toast. "She shouldn't be going anywhere."

Katherine said nothing, but gave him a glance that told him she didn't agree. The look he shot back that said he didn't care what she thought. It occurred to him that they'd been having this nonverbal communication since he was four and she was eight. Their mother had emphasized peace in the family, so they'd conducted all their arguments when she wasn't around. In her presence, they'd simply glared at each other.

"I'll call Ben after breakfast," Drew said, taking his plate and joining them, "and you can hear it from him."

The phone rang, as though the very mention of a call had made one materialize. Drew went to the wall phone near the stove and grinned when Ben announced himself.

"I thought I'd look in on Jeanie and the baby this afternoon," Ben said.

"I'd appreciate that." Drew smiled at Jeanie and his sister. "We were just talking about your order that Jeanie and the baby stay quiet for a couple of days."

"Did I say that?" Ben asked. "Or are you just trying to keep a beautiful woman nearby?"

"Yes," Drew replied with a smile for Jeanie's benefit. "I think it's a good idea, too. So what time can we expect you?"

"Soon as I can make it. Probably between two and three."

"Okay. Thanks, Ben."

Drew resumed his place at the table and told Jeanie Ben was coming.

She nodded. At least she wouldn't leave until Ben had seen her.

Jeremy awoke just as Jeanie finished breakfast, and she took him into the bedroom to nurse him.

Katherine pounced on the opportunity to talk privately. Or rather, criticize privately.

"*What* are you doing?" she demanded in a low voice, pointing her knife and fork heavenward to underline her disbelief. "Her story does not ring true."

Drew grinned at her. "No kidding. But the part about the baby is true. I helped at the birth." He got up to get the coffeepot.

"I don't mean the baby," she retorted impatiently, "I mean the Mafia stuff. And if you don't believe her either, why are you letting her stay here? If she is on the run, it's probably from the law!"

He topped up her coffee. "Come on, Katherine. Does she seem like the criminal type to you?"

"For God's sake, Drew. Even criminals never seem like the criminal type, otherwise people wouldn't be taken in by them so easily."

"You've been watching too many movies."

"And you're too trusting."

He studied his older sister, half filled with admiration for her, and half annoyed with her. "You know, the fact that I had to pay *you* to let me help you mow lawns when we were kids doesn't mean I was too trusting, it means you were willing to exploit your loving and helpful little brother. It's your problem, not mine."

She pressed her lips together to prevent a smile and swatted his shoulder. "I'm serious."

"So am I. I was the best flower-bed weeder you ever had." His sister closed her eyes, obviously summoning patience, then pinned him with another look—this one pleading and concerned. "If she brings trouble to this family with Daddy just getting out of prison…"

"Katherine." Drew placed his hand over hers on the table. "She's my responsibility, and I'll make sure no one gets hurt. If there's trouble, *she's* the one in it, and I can't just throw her out."

"When I walked in, it sounded like she wanted to leave."

"Her baby is nine hours old, Katherine."

She shot out of her chair. "You are just like Dad! Always so in charge, so confident, and look where it got him! I think he didn't fight to prove his innocence because he was so shocked to discover he could be vulnerable like everyone else. He and Uncle Ken and Uncle Jonathan thought they were invincible, and then what happened?"

She didn't wait for an answer.

"Daddy went to jail for selling military secrets, Uncle Jonathan died, and Uncle Ken got divorced and can't seem to find the right woman." She realized she was shouting and cleared her throat to add more quietly, "That's what comes of thinking you know it all. Or can do it all. Tragedy."

"You know it all and can do it all, all the time," he countered, pushing his chair back to stand and wrap her in a hug. "Relax, Katherine. It's been bad, but the good part's coming. Don't give up yet."

He felt her lean against him and return his hug. "It's just…Dad's been gone so long, you know?"

"I know."

Katherine had been ten when their father went to prison, and she'd dedicated her life ever since to helping their mother cope.

Helen Kinard sold their elegant home on Forrester Square, where all three partners of NorPac and Eagle Aerotech had lived, and moved with her children to a far less elegant Seattle suburb. Shortly after, she went back to teaching. Drew hadn't noticed the family's reduced circumstances; his life had been all about his bicycle and toy trucks and he still had those.

But Katherine had been ten, and he remembered that she'd willingly given up her dance and gymnastics classes to help save money, and she'd been very serious about the lawn-mowing business she started. She'd been in her glory because it allowed her to make money and look after Drew at the same time.

As an adult, she'd as much as given up a social life to work hard and help their mother, and keep her too busy to pine for their father. And she'd saved all her extra money to open a day-care center. She was the poster woman for the Rome-wasn't-built-in-a-day principle. His sister had more patience and determination than anyone Drew knew.

"Do you think they're going to be okay?" she asked worriedly, her eyes dark with concern.

"You mean Mom and Dad?"

"Yes. Mom's dreamed of his coming home for so long, I just hope…you know…that the spark's still there."

He'd seen his father watch their mother on visiting day. He'd listened to Louis Kinard pleading over and over for Drew to take good care of her. It was still there.

"I have no doubt," Drew assured her. "I think you're worried about them because their reconnecting is going to free you up to worry about your own life."

She drew a breath, her concern apparently put aside for the moment. "Not a chance. I'm going to be too busy for the next few years getting the day care on its feet and paying back all my loans."

"I thought the loan from Jordan Edwards had no interest and no due date." Jordan was their father's friend and had believed in his innocence all along. According to Drew's mother, he had helped her make the mortgage payment a time or two when money was tight.

Several times a year, when Drew was in college, Jordan sent him spending money, and he'd come forward eagerly to help Katherine establish her business.

"And for that kindness," she said, "I'd like to pay him back as quickly as possible. And don't forget, I've got Carlos to fill my life."

He nodded. "Carlos is great and we all love him, but you need a romantic relationship, sis. Someone to make you remember that you're young and beautiful."

It amused him that she became embarrassed, then upset him that her eyes filled with tears. Their father's impending homecoming and the opening of her business were making her emotional.

He took that as a sign to lighten up. "Of course,

if you did fall in love with somebody," he said, "we'd have to pay him big bucks to take you off our hands. Maybe even tie a pair of Mariners tickets around your neck as a bonus."

She gave him a playful shove and picked up her bakery box and clipboard. "I'm sure the staff will enjoy these. Mom and I are going to visit Dad this afternoon. Do you want to come? Mom's coming from a luncheon, so she's going to meet me there. If you want to ride with me, we can discuss the opening in the car."

"Sure," he replied. "What time?"

"Can you meet me in my office at one?"

"I'll be there."

She turned to leave and came face-to-face with Jeanie, who held a fussing baby in her arms.

"It was nice to meet you, Katherine," Jeanie said.

Katherine patted the baby's back. "You, too." She headed for the elevator. "See you at one!" she shouted back to Drew.

The elevator light pinged, the door opened, and she disappeared inside.

JULIA PATTED Jeremy's back and watched Drew clear the table. She was upset by what she'd overheard. He and Katherine had lived much of their lives with their father serving time in prison. That must have been difficult.

As he turned from the table, a stack of dishes in hand, he noticed her expression and must have guessed what she was thinking.

"Just ignore Katherine," he said, misinterpreting

her concern. "She didn't know there was Mafia in Seattle."

He filled the dishwasher without looking up at her. It was hard to tell if his comment was intended to needle her or not.

"They're everywhere," she said, trying to sound like an expert on the subject. "Who do you think runs the docks and the gambling that goes on in the back rooms of the music clubs?" She had no idea if there was gambling in the clubs, but she thought it sounded good.

He looked up at that, his eyes unreadable. They held hers for a moment and she was convinced he suspected her story was a crock.

"No idea," he said finally, putting detergent into the dishwasher.

Julia rocked the baby from side to side. "This must look very suspicious to her," she said matter-of-factly, hoping to convince him of her sincerity by confronting his doubts—or Katherine's. "I understand why she's concerned for you. It must have been difficult for your family with your father in prison."

He shrugged that off. "We survived."

"I'm sure it was harder than you make it sound."

"Yeah, it was," he agreed, closing the dishwasher door and setting the controls. "But now that he's coming home, I'd just as soon forget it. Katherine and I are going to visit him this afternoon. Promise me you won't run off until Ben's had a chance to make sure you and the baby are all right."

"I'm not going to run off before you come home," she promised. "But when he says we're both fine,

I'm leaving. I so appreciate all you've done for us, but I have to go.''

"We can talk about that tonight.''

"You don't get to talk about it,'' she said, smiling but firm. "It's my decision. But thank you for everything.''

He raised an eyebrow at her pontifical tone but replied simply, "You're welcome." Then he excused himself to go into his office.

She walked into the living room with the baby, patting his back and relishing the warmth of his tiny body against her shoulder. It was astonishing how much had changed in the past ten hours. Jeremy's gentle weight felt like an anchor, stabilizing her in a life that had tossed her around, taking loved ones from her, shocking her to the core, sending her on the run.

After last night's rain, sun poured through the living room windows of Drew's apartment and pinned her to a shaft of light in the middle of a light blue carpet. Given a choice, she thought in a moment of self-indulgence, she'd stay right here.

But she couldn't afford to be self-indulgent. She had to think of the potential threat she posed to Drew and the children in the day care downstairs, and to the safety of her baby. Once Ben Jessup declared her and Jeremy healthy, she had to leave.

CHAPTER FOUR

KATHERINE WAS NERVOUS. Drew could tell because she was chatty. His sister was usually able to convey her ideas with an economy of words, but today she was rambling on about things she wanted repaired or built for the grand opening. She posed questions then answered them herself without waiting for his thoughts. Drew simply leaned back in the front seat of her classic '74 light blue VW Beetle and enjoyed her small lapse of control.

They were ten miles from the Northwest Correctional Facility when she finally became aware that she'd been talking for twenty minutes straight.

"Geez," she groaned, passing a truck and settling into the outside lane, "why didn't you tell me to shut up!"

He grinned at her. "I tried, but you were waxing poetic about playground equipment and you didn't hear me."

"I'm sorry." She expelled a ragged breath. "I guess I'm nervous about Dad coming home."

"Why?" he asked gently. "You're not still worried about him and Mom getting along?"

She frowned at the road. "No. I guess I just feel...I don't know. Less than I should, maybe. I mean, I remember how much he adored me. I was daddy's little girl and I loved it. In all the years we've visited him, I've put on this front of woman-in-control—even when I was just a kid. I wanted him to believe that I was taking care of Mom and you and that everything would be fine until he came home.''

He turned toward her, a little surprised by the serious concern in her voice. He bridged the space between their seats by putting a hand on her shoulder. ''But you did take care of us and everything is fine. Why are you worried?''

With one hand she made a helpless gesture. ''No man in my life, no grandchildren for him to come home to, no big successes.''

''What about the day care,'' he pointed out, ''and the fact that everyone loves you? Those are successes.''

''The day care's just starting out,'' she argued, ''and so far all I've accomplished with it is to incur a mountain of debt. And if everyone does love me, it's because I'm Helen Kinard's daughter and everyone loves *her*.''

''Kathy!'' he chided, calling her by the childhood name no one was allowed to use but their mother. ''You've been open two weeks and you have an enrollment of fifty. Jordan Edwards trusted you enough to lend you a small fortune for an unlimited time. And people do love Mom, but they love you because you're warm and cheerful and completely competent. So knock it off. You have no reason to suddenly develop insecurities. God, the number of times you've bossed me around...''

"Okay!" She pinched his finger on her shoulder and cast him a quick, smiling glance. "Thank you. It's just weird, you know. We're going to have a father again. I mean, a father who's actually there."

It *was* weird, but he kept all his own insecurities in check.

The prison was audibly depressing as well as a visual downer, Drew thought as he and Katherine followed a guard to the visiting area. The unyielding gray stone was a grim sight, but lately the clang of iron locking behind him in every doorway was even more disturbing and deepened the anguish he felt for his father.

Louis Kinard, however, always surprised him by looking remarkably normal when he walked into the room to sit around the table with his family. And today was no different.

His father was sixty-two, just under six feet tall, and fit from spending all his spare time in the facility's gym. His dark hair had grown gray, and though twenty years spent behind bars for a crime he hadn't committed didn't show in his body, it was visible in his eyes. There was no rage or resentment there, but a definite sadness that was most prevalent when he looked upon his children.

"Hi, Dad!" Katherine wrapped her arms around him and held him tightly. Her voice was cheerful, belying the worries she'd shared with Drew in the car. She stepped back to look at him. "I can't believe you'll be home in less than a month! Have you started packing?"

Their father laughed as she'd intended him to.

"That won't take too much time. Drew." His father moved past Katherine to take Drew into his arms. "How are you, son?"

"Great," Drew replied, comforted by the strength of his father's embrace. "You're looking good, Dad."

His father held him at arm's length. "You, too, son. Where's your mother?"

"She's coming from a luncheon," Katherine explained as they took a seat around the table, "so she drove her own car."

Louis winced. "Has her driving improved any?"

"She hasn't gone through the garage door lately," Drew said.

Katherine looked from one to the other, her lips pursed disapprovingly. "It was a faulty garage door opener."

"We didn't even have a garage door opener when she ran over my bike," Drew said.

Katherine shook her head. "That was fifteen years ago!"

"Doesn't matter," he teased. "My bike wasn't even in the driveway—it was on the lawn."

His father laughed. "She always did take the most direct route everywhere."

Even Katherine began to smile. The teasing about Helen's driving had been a harmless way to pretend that they were any other family, laughing together about the foibles of one of their members.

"Just asking," Louis said blandly, "because if she drives up into the prison laundry or the exercise yard, they might add another year to my time."

That was almost funny, but not quite.

Katherine handed her father the magazine she'd tucked in her satchel.

"What's this?" he asked, glancing at the celebrity on the cover. "*Gentlemen's Quarterly*?"

"I thought you might want me to buy you some clothes for when you get out." When he looked up at her in surprise, she shrugged and added a little defensively, "You were always well-dressed. And I know a few outlets where we can get you some great stuff. I'll buy you a few things to have when you come out, then take you shopping for a complete wardrobe later."

"*GQ*." Drew repeated the name of the magazine with a slightly scornful note in his voice. He went around the table to look over his father's shoulder as Louis turned the pages. "Get serious, Katherine."

His father pulled him down beside him. "Sit down and be quiet. You could use a little sharpening up, too."

"Hey!"

His father cast a mildly judgmental glance over Drew's appearance. "Denim and fleece were fine when you were a struggling student, but now that you're getting a name as an architect, you need some style."

Drew looked down at his jeans and Washington State University sweatshirt. "I'm just…trying to stay humble," he said. "And these are my *good* jeans."

His father and Katherine rolled their eyes.

"Drew," Louis said patiently, "I look more fashionable than you do and I'm in prison."

Drew pretended to be hurt. "That's because the chambray shirt is classic. And the stenciled numbers on the back add a certain street-style that happens to be popular right now."

Louis laughed.

The door opened suddenly and Helen Kinard was admitted. His mother looked very smart, Drew thought, in lavender pants and top that left little doubt about her dedication to chic. On her left shoulder was a diamond butterfly pin Louis had given her in better days.

Louis rose from the table and opened his arms. She walked into them as though they hadn't been separated by distance and prison bars for twenty years. Drew saw Katherine bite her lip and feign interest in the magazine and a sullen-looking model in a white shirt with puffy sleeves that Drew would wear only if rendered unconscious.

"Who would wear that?" he demanded, leaning over the magazine from the opposite side, hoping to distract her from her emotion. Something was going on with her today that he didn't entirely understand.

She gave him a scornful glance and turned the page. "No one," she replied, "but I was thinking this looks like you." She pointed to the photo of another model with obvious anger issues. He wore beige slacks and a navy-and-beige-striped sweater. "It's casual without being slummy."

He took offense to that. "I don't look slummy."

"No, but you always look as though you're on your way to help somebody paint their house or garden."

"Nobody paints their garden," he said without

looking up at her. He knew what she meant, but their parents were still holding each other, and emotion stretched tightly all around them.

She punched his shoulder. "Paint their house," she repeated, enunciating carefully, "or do their gardening."

"Good Lord," his mother said, indicating Drew and Katherine as she drew out of her husband's arms, "are they squabbling again? Maybe I could just leave them with you and you could find cells for them on opposite ends of the block. I swear, they can't be together for two minutes without quarreling about something."

"It's your fault," Katherine said, straightening up to receive their mother's hug. "If you'd given him away like I suggested when he drove my doll carriage into the pool, we wouldn't have to deal with him now."

Louis grinned as he and Helen sat close together. "Well, your mother had a fondness for him."

Drew grinned, too. "She liked to run over my bicycle."

Helen raised her eyes to heaven. "How long does it take to be forgiven for a crime in this family?" Then realizing what she'd said, she looked from her husband to her children in openmouthed dismay.

"In my experience," Louis replied with a straight face, "twenty years."

Helen wrapped her arms around his neck. "Oh, stop it. It's not funny. You didn't commit any crime. God, I can't wait for you to come home."

Her voice broke as she leaned into him. Louis held

her for a moment, then slapped a hand down on the magazine. "Katherine's trying to get me to pick out some things I like so that she can buy me a change of clothes to come home in. And maybe encourage Drew to look less like a reprobate and more like an upwardly mobile professional."

Happy for the distraction, Helen pored through the magazine with them.

It was almost time for their visit to end when Katherine finally forced her father to pick something he liked. She reached across the table to give him a hug.

"I'll be back with a few things next week," she said, "and if you don't like them, I'll try again." Then she hugged her mother. "We're meeting for lunch with Jordan on Friday, right?"

Helen nodded. "Noon. It's on my calendar."

"Okay. I'll see you then, unless you want to come by and lend a hand on Wednesday. Carmen, our head teacher, has a dentist appointment in the afternoon and it'll leave us a little shorthanded."

"I'll be there."

Drew hugged his mother and shook hands with his father.

"Go shopping with your sister," his mother said, her tone almost pleading. "If you're going to be a man of business, you should look...more..." Her eyes ran over his ultracasual attire and she finally said diplomatically, "More put together."

"Come on," Drew said, turning from his mother to his father. "Have you really found me offensive to look at all this time?"

"Yes, we have." Katherine took his arm. "All this

time. Now, let's get a move on. Bye, Mom. Bye, Dad.''

Drew was still protesting when the guard opened the door to let them through. "I can't believe—" he began.

"Oh, stop," Katherine said, pulling on him. "You dress so badly that if I didn't have a hold of you, they'd put you in a cell, it's such a crime. There wouldn't even be a trial."

"I'm not going shopping with you."

"Your cute little waif-mother knows how to dress."

He frowned at his sister as they walked through another door, opened for them by a guard. "She was wearing a sweatsuit. Big deal."

She looked at him pityingly. "A very, *very* expensive sweatsuit."

"I didn't know that."

"I'm not surprised."

They were halfway home before they spoke again.

"Tell me about Jeanie," Katherine said as she found a comfortable spot in the slow lane.

"What I know about her is what I told you," he said, glancing at his watch. It was just after three. Ben would be with her and the baby now.

"You don't believe the Mafia stuff."

"No."

"Then you're deliberately playing with fire?"

He turned to her with an impatient look. "I'm not playing with anything. She's all alone with a brand-new baby and something or someone is threatening her. I'm just providing a safe harbor."

"She lied to you!"

"She'll tell me the truth eventually."

"Why does it matter?"

He didn't know the answer to that. "I'm not sure. Because she's very brave, I guess."

"Brave and dishonest."

He remembered thinking at four years old how satisfying it would be to push Katherine into the pool. She'd been eight and had embarrassed him in front of his friends by bodily pulling him away from a tree they'd all climbed to stop him from joining them. But sensing that giving her a strategic shove would have gotten him into trouble, he'd settled for throwing her doll carriage in the pool instead.

He'd still been punished, but it had been worth it.

He felt the same way now.

"Katherine," he said firmly, "Jeanie is none of your business, okay?"

"I'm not just being nosy!" she protested. "I…"

"You don't think you are," he disputed. "You think you're being protective. But if I don't want your protection, then you're just being nosy."

"You're just being stubborn. And you might remember that even though she's lying about the Mafia, she could be married to someone."

"Kathy…"

"Okay. Just don't come crying to me when she breaks your heart."

He closed his eyes and prayed for patience. "My heart isn't involved, sis. She needed help and I gave it to her. That's all."

"Your heart's always involved," she insisted. "It's

the way you are. You're a very unusual man. Stupid, but unusual.''

''I love you, too.''

''Oh, shut up and let me concentrate on my driving.''

''What's to concentrate on? You're in the geezer lane doing thirty. What could happen? We might get run over by a street sweeper, but that's about it.''

She grinned reluctantly. ''Not my fault. Mom taught me to drive.''

They laughed together and the argument was forgotten.

''What do you think about giving them a couple of days in a hotel out of town—maybe up in Canada—when Dad gets out? So they can spend some time together without the press asking questions and people gawking.''

She glanced at him in pleased surprise. ''That's brilliant, Drew.''

''I was thinking Victoria would isolate them a little.''

''Perfect! I'm swamped. Do you have time to make reservations?''

''Sure. A hotel or a B&B?''

She frowned as she considered. ''A B&B's more intimate.''

''True. But you can get room service even in the middle of the night at a hotel.''

''You're the only one who eats in the middle of the night.''

''Then a B&B it is.''

''They'll love it, I think. I know they haven't lost

their closeness, but living apart like that is so unnatural. Coming together again after all these years has got to make them both nervous.''

''You're right, but Mom's so steady, and Dad loves her so much. They'll be fine.''

She gave him one of those looks he was more used to. The one that said he didn't know anything, and she, being older, was the wiser, more superior being.

''It's nice that you're an optimist, Drew,'' she said, ''but what do you know about married love? This adjustment you take so casually might be really hard for them.''

He shook his head at her as they turned off the busy highway and into a mall. ''If they adjusted to the dark reality of his being in jail and the long separation that meant, I'm sure they can readjust to being together again.''

''But twenty years have passed! They're different people. Mom's held the family together on her own. And he's probably seen and heard things none of us would want to know about.''

''It occurs to me,'' he said gently but firmly, ''that you're worrying about them so you don't have to worry about you. Get a life, Katherine, and don't get in their way.''

She found a parking spot in front of a men's store, brought the car to a stop, then turned to him, clearly affronted.

''I have no intention of getting in their way!''

''Well, I hope not,'' he said, ''because they seem to me to be excited and anxious for his return home. Don't share your doubts with them and give them second thoughts about something they're probably going to have to rely on instinct to get through anyway.''

She swatted his shoulder with the magazine. ''I wouldn't do that!''

''Good.'' He looked at the mall and asked, ''Why are we here?''

''I thought we could pick out some clothes for Dad together.''

''Now? He won't be out for almost a month.''

She rolled her eyes. ''A good wardrobe takes planning. I know you don't understand that, but trust me on it. And we may not be able to coordinate our schedules again to get the same few hours off. Please indulge me.''

''That's it,'' he said, unbuckling his seat belt and opening his door. ''I'm finding you a man. If I'm going to have to start shopping with you, you're getting a husband if I have to search one out for you myself.''

''YOU'RE BOTH DOING WELL,'' Ben Jessup said after examining Julia and Jeremy, ''but the baby seems a little distraught.''

He'd been screaming most of the afternoon and Julia had no idea what to do. All her attempts to pacify him had failed.

''He seems to be eating okay,'' she said, feeling depressed. ''I think he just doesn't like me. Now that he's seen me, he wants back in the womb.''

Ben laughed. ''It's more likely that he's picking up a little tension from you. Are you in pain?''

She shook her head quickly. "I'm fine, Dr. Jessup. I guess I'm just a little worried about…" Unable to explain everything that was wrong in her life, she simply expressed it with a wave of her hand. "You know."

"Your…husband?"

"Yes," she lied.

"No one can fix your problems but you, Jeanie."

"Yes, I know." They were talking about different things, of course, but she couldn't fix her real problems until she'd heard from Chloe, and Chloe hadn't called. Julia refused to even entertain the thought that her friend hadn't escaped Pike Place Market.

She had begun to wonder about the sanity of their plan, though. It had sounded doable when they'd conceived it; now she wasn't so sure.

"But I wouldn't worry about that right now," the doctor said, taking the screaming baby from her and bouncing him in his arm. "You have a nice, safe place to stay, so maybe you should just try to relax here until you feel stronger and the baby's more accustomed to his new world. You shouldn't make major decisions about your life while your hormones are rioting. Just lie low until life evens out."

Miraculously, the baby stopped crying.

"How'd you do that?" Julia demanded.

"Experience," he said with a smile. "Remember, I'm a father. Even though Doug's already two and a half, he can still keep me up nights if he's eaten the wrong thing or caught a cold."

"Doug's a lucky little guy. His father always

knows what to do. Poor Jeremy has a mother who's afraid of him.''

Ben handed the baby back to her. ''Now, that's silly. At this age, he's operating on sensation rather than thought, so just hold him snugly and let him *believe* you know what you're doing, even if you don't. He'll relax. And pretty soon you'll gain a little confidence, too. Be patient with yourself, and he'll be patient with you.''

He was the nicest man, Julia thought. ''Your wife is so lucky,'' she said, taking the baby back from him. Jeremy seemed to be asleep again.

She looked up at Ben Jessup, about to thank him for all he'd done, when she noticed the grim expression on his face.

''Actually, she's not very lucky,'' he countered. ''She died of cancer two years ago.''

Julia closed her eyes regretfully. ''I'm so sorry.''

''Don't be.'' He forced a smile and packed up his things. ''We had a good life together, if only briefly. We wanted a lot of children, but we started late and had difficulty conceiving. Then Doug finally came along.''

As she held her own baby, Julia could appreciate the unutterable sadness of a mother separated from her child.

''I'm so sorry,'' she said again. They were the only words that seemed to fit.

''Thank you.'' He started for the door and she followed.

''Want me to act as your matchmaker?'' she asked,

partly to lighten the mood, and partly because she hated the thought of him and his son alone.

He stopped at the elevator and gave a little laugh. "Thanks, but that's a job I really should do myself. I want to get married again, but the woman has to be the right one. Doug's very special."

She patted his arm. "So are you. Thanks for all you've done for us. I don't know what I'd have done—or Drew, for that matter—if you hadn't come to help us last night."

He shrugged a shoulder. "That's what friends are for. Particularly pediatrician friends."

"Thanks again, Dr. Jessup."

"Call me if there's a problem," he advised. "Otherwise, I'll see you in a week."

A week. She wondered where she'd be in a week. She smiled and hoped he'd take that for assent.

When the elevator door closed behind him, she put Jeremy down in his basket and tidied up a little. She took two messages from prospective clients, and one from a young woman who giggled a lot, wanted to know when Drew would be back and asked who Julia was.

"Just a friend dropping off a casserole," she fibbed. She certainly was becoming adept at lying.

"I thought he was a good cook," the woman said, suspicion suddenly overtaking the giggles.

Annoyed and inexplicably provoked, Julia replied, "He is, but he says nothing makes him as happy as my chili and corn-bread casserole. I'll tell him you called, Tallulah."

"It's Toria!"

Julia made that small correction on the message pad and hung up the phone.

When the phone rang again, Julia was certain it was Toria taking issue with her casserole, but it was one of the women at the day care downstairs.

"I'm Angela Gilmore," she said. Her voice was cheerful and warm. "I work with infants. Katherine asked me to call you when my last charge was gone to see if you needed help with your baby."

"That's so thoughtful, thank you. Dr. Jessup helped me a little, but I still feel like I'm all thumbs."

"Shall I come up and show you how to give him a bath? That usually makes mom and baby feel better."

"Aren't you anxious to go home?"

"No, all that's waiting for me there is laundry and breakfast dishes. I'll be right up."

Good thing, too, Julia thought as she hung up the phone. Jeremy was awake again and crying pathetically.

Angela Gilmore was average in height with graying dark hair. The very short cut accentuated warm dark eyes and smooth skin remarkably free of wrinkles for a woman who had to be in her mid-fifties. A pair of glasses hung on a chain around her neck and she slipped them on now for a closer look at Julia and the squalling baby.

"You're a handsome little fellow," she said as she reached for Jeremy with the air of an expert. He continued to cry, however. "Katherine didn't tell me much. Are you and Drew..." She made a walking gesture with her index and middle finger. Julia guessed that meant romantically involved.

"No," she replied quickly, afraid of besmirching the reputation of her host. She didn't want anyone taking gossip back to the day care that she'd had Drew's baby. "I'd never seen Drew until yesterday. I'm…escaping an abusive husband, and I guess the stress of being on the run made me go into labor."

A score of questions rose up in Angela's eyes. Were you escaping an abusive husband on foot? How did you end up in Belltown? Why are you still here?

But the older woman asked none of them and headed into the bathroom. She ran warm water into the small plastic basin she'd brought with her, along with a particularly soft white washcloth and bath towel.

"During the first week," she said, placing Jeremy on the bath towel on the bathroom counter, "all you really need to do is sponge bathe him with warm water." She glanced at Julia with a smile. "We do what we call 'topping and tailing.' You wash the face and the folds of the neck with extra care because milk can sometimes hide in there and cause a rash."

Angela showed Julia how to wash the baby, then Julia put a hand on the baby to keep him still while Angela rinsed out the cloth and worked carefully around the umbilical stump. Next she cleaned Jeremy's bottom. "Make sure you get in all the little folds and crevices here, too. The stump will probably stay on for about a week, and though it looks like it might hurt, most babies don't even seem to notice it."

She dug into a pocket for a packaged alcohol wipe,

which she removed and dabbed around the area. "That's all you have to do for it unless it gets red and looks infected. A little bleeding is normal as it begins to fall off, so don't worry about that. There."

She wiped Jeremy's face and bottom with the other end of the towel, then handed him back to Julia. "Just a new diaper and a clean T-shirt, and he should be fine. Next week, if you're ready for it, I can show you how to bathe him in a little baby tub. Or you can take him into your bathtub, if there's someone around to help you."

Next week. Julia had no idea where he would even be in seven days' time.

But Jeremy was quiet and sweet smelling, and she accepted that she had to live her life from day to day and take pleasure in the small victories—like a bathed and seemingly contented baby. Next week would have to take care of itself.

"Angela," she said sincerely, "you're a lifesaver."

Angela shrugged off her praise. "You're welcome to come downstairs with him anytime if you don't know what to do. Or just call, and if we're not in the middle of our own crisis, one of us will come up and help."

Julia hugged her; she couldn't help herself. She felt great relief at the knowledge that help was close at hand. Drew was wonderful, but he knew even less about babies than she did.

"I owe you big-time."

"Well..." Angela waggled her eyebrows playfully. "If you really feel that way, Hy Berg makes the best caramel fudge latte in the whole world. One day when you're feeling strong enough to go out, you can bring me one.''

Julia raised an eyebrow. ''What's High Berg?''

Angela walked to the door, her arm around Julia and Jeremy. ''He's a who, Jeanie. Hyram Berg. He owns the coffee shop next door—Caffeine Hy's. He says his business has tripled since Katherine opened the day care. Parents dropping off babies and picking up coffee drinks, parents picking up babies and coffee drinks, staff running over on their breaks, Katherine running an intravenous line from his place into her office.''

Julia laughed at that silly mental image.

''If you like coffee,'' Angela said, pushing the elevator button, ''you have to go to Hy's. Tell him you live in this building and you'll get special treatment.''

Julia had a sudden and desperate need for a mocha, double tall, double cream, with chocolate jimmies.

''Thanks so much again, Angela,'' she said as the elevator arrived.

''You're welcome!'' Angela waved as the door closed on her.

Julia smiled down at Jeremy, who lay quietly in her arms, his pruny little face absolutely angelic. ''I'm going to learn to do this,'' she promised, ''and before you know it, I'm going to be the best mother you've ever seen. Well, I know you haven't seen anyone but me, but you can take my word for it. You're going to be happy and safe. Is that clear?''

It must have been. Jeremy didn't stir.

CHAPTER FIVE

DREW ARRIVED HOME with Chinese takeout and a two-liter carton of milk. He thought Jeanie looked a little less stressed, and even somewhat glad to see him.

She sat at the kitchen table, the baby in her arms, as he put everything in the middle, brought two plates from the cupboard, and poured the milk into two tall glasses.

He leaned over her shoulder to touch the baby's wild spiked hair.

"He's looking good," he said, catching a whiff of her fresh floral fragrance. "And so are you." Her hair was glossy and piled loosely on top of her head.

"Thank you. I took a shower and washed my hair while Jeremy slept. It felt so good."

"What did Ben say?"

"He said we're both doing fine."

He was glad to hear that, but knew it meant she considered herself free to leave. She looked a little hesitant as he handed her the take-out box of spring rolls—as though she was reluctant to approach a subject she knew he wouldn't like.

In the very brief time he'd spent with her, he'd already learned that the quickest way to alienate her was to stand between her and whatever it was she wanted to do.

"So when are you leaving?" he asked, determined to take the wind out of her sails. He held up a container, offering to serve her. "Broccoli beef?" he asked.

She looked surprised for a moment, then pushed her plate toward him. "Yes, please," she replied.

"Sesame chicken?"

"Yes."

"Kung Pao shrimp?"

"Ah...no. Too hot for the baby, I think."

"Right. I forgot that. Fried rice? Pan-fried noodles?"

"Yes and yes!" she said with enthusiasm. "Fattening carbs are my favorite thing."

"Great." He spooned the food onto her plate, then his own. When he looked up again, she was watching him speculatively. He maintained his nonchalance with great care.

"Won tons?" he asked, holding out the last box.

She hesitated a moment, then reached for one. The baby stirred a little, but remained asleep.

"Ben suggested I stay for a few days," she said conversationally, dropping a won ton onto her plate. She glanced at him quickly, then away, reaching back into the box for a small container of plum sauce. "He thought the baby was crying because I was upsetting him."

He frowned solicitously. "But you've been so careful..."

She cut him off with a nod. "He thought Jeremy might be picking up on my insecurities."

"You two probably forged quite a bond while you were pregnant with him. I'll bet he reads you as well as you're trying to read him."

"Maybe even better. He's not confused by outside stuff."

"Are you confused?"

She blew air between her lips in a very unladylike way and nodded emphatically. "Yes. My life's taken a big turn, and now I have someone else to consider, not just myself." She leveled a steady gaze at him and asked gravely, "*Would* it be all right if we stayed for a few days? Just until Jeremy mellows out?"

"I thought I suggested that this morning."

She made a face at him. "I had to hear it from someone with a medical degree."

"Of course you can stay," he said, feeling himself relax. He didn't know why he should. His relatively quiet, but very satisfying, life had been disrupted by a baby and a woman who was lying to him, and he was asking to prolong the disturbance?

He had a suspicion this wasn't at all wise, but then he'd always maintained, despite his protective mother and sister, that life couldn't be experienced if the only criterion for whether or not to take an action was the wisdom of it.

"You're sure?" she asked, wide-eyed and sincerely concerned. "I mean, you've done so much for us already, and you have your own life and a business...oh!"

She got up from the table and went to the counter,

where she picked up the message pad near the phone. She handed it to him, then sat down carefully. "That Mitchell person wants to talk to you about remodeling an old house into law offices, and James Cranston wasn't specific, but I happen to know he's the lawyer for the Wyatts."

Drew scanned the list and raised an inquiring eyebrow. "The Wyatts?"

"He's a cannery heir, and she's a former dancer, now a patron of the arts. For a couple of years they've been talking about building a theater on a waterfront property they have in Bellevue."

"Your husband has interesting connections," he said, surprised that she knew so much about the couple.

She shook her head. "They're my own connections. I went to school with Marissa Wyatt, their daughter. You must have made a good impression on someone. The Wyatts do everything elegantly and spare no expense."

He had to smile at that. "That's good to know. I'd love an income that would allow me an office that *isn't* above a day care where babies are sleeping."

"Do you tend to pace noisily when you're thinking?"

"Sometimes. I also shout when I'm angry, love reggae music, and clog dancing."

She blinked at him over a forkful of fried rice. "I don't believe you!"

"Okay," he admitted, "I lied about the clog dancing."

"I mean I don't believe that you shout."

"You'll have to talk to Katherine. She'll tell you that I'm not the saintly paragon I appear to be."

"I'd have to see it for myself," she insisted. Then her expression softened and she asked gently, "How was your dad?"

Drew was surprised by the sudden change in subject, but she did seem genuinely interested. "Uh... fine. Well, as fine as he can be under the circumstances. But he's looking forward to coming home."

"Your mom must be thrilled."

He smiled fondly as he thought of his mother. "She is. She's been a brick for all of us all this time. I'd like to see her really happy again."

"What kind of work did your father do?"

"He was in partnership with two of his friends in the aircraft industry, then later they developed software that had military applications. That's how he ended up in jail. Someone set him up to make it look as though he'd sold some of their designs on the black market. He denied it, but the evidence was overwhelming."

"How awful." She sighed. "I know what it's like to feel alone. It must have been like that sometimes for you, too, even though you had your mother and sister."

He nodded. "It was, and I'd feel very sorry for myself, but my mom kept going and my sister was like this whirlwind of activity to make extra money to help out, so it was hard to mope. No one was paying attention." He grinned. "So I had to toughen up and work hard, too. It made the three of us even closer, because everything we did was aimed at making sure Dad didn't worry about us.''

DREW'S FAMILY SOUNDED WONDERFUL to Julia. Her uncle had seldom had time for her, and had left her in the care of a long line of housekeepers who came and went. A lonely child, she'd wanted desperately to connect with him, to feel that he really wanted her, wanted to know her. But it had never happened.

When she'd graduated from college with a degree in political science and learned he intended to run for office, she'd volunteered to manage his campaign, certain that would bring them closer together. But while her uncle had seemed to appreciate her efforts on his behalf, he never seemed to appreciate her.

He'd also taken an instant dislike to Devon, which she'd never understood. Devon had been so affable, it was hard to imagine anyone not enjoying his company.

She'd almost been afraid to form the thought, but she'd wondered if her uncle had been afraid that if she married, his line to ready cash would be cut off. The generous monthly allowance provided by her trust fund supported the household and paid his secretary and driver. Randolph Stanton was an attorney, but hadn't practiced since his election two years earlier. She guessed that his salary as a senator supported his trips to Barbados.

"What're you thinking?" Drew asked, snapping her out of her thoughts. He sounded concerned. "By the looks of that frown, you're going to give yourself indigestion.'' His gaze narrowed on her. ''You worried about your husband?''

She suddenly hated her deception. It had been intended to keep her safe, but now it couldn't help but pose a threat to the growing friendship between her and Drew. She was fairly sure he suspected she was lying, but though she trusted Drew, she couldn't risk confiding in him—for his own safety and for the baby's. Her best bet was to simply lie low, gain strength and help her baby grow strong, then walk out of Drew's life before he ever had to know what she'd done.

''A little. But I'm sure he has no idea where I am. Worrying's just a habit of mine.''

''I can see why,'' he said. The remark was loaded, but she couldn't get into it now.

''Jeremy and I are just going to rest up for a few days, then get a lawyer and get Marco out of my life.''

He smiled his approval. ''Good plan. And I happen to know a very good lawyer. When you feel up to it, I can introduce you.''

She'd be gone by then, thank God. ''Thank you. Can I have another spring roll?''

He looked into the box and shook his head gravely. ''Sorry. It's the last one.''

She wasn't sure if was he teasing her or not. Then she saw the gleam of humor in his eyes. ''That's not very heroic,'' she accused with a straight face.

He raised an eyebrow. ''I didn't realize there was heroism involved in spring rolls.''

''Well, of course there is,'' she stated gravely.

"There's heroism involved in everything. Giving up something you want so someone who needs it can have it is heroic."

"You may want it, but I'm not sure you *need* it."

"I'm trying to regain my strength." That, too, she said without blinking.

He waved the message pad at her. "So am I. I have to be strong and clever to do my work."

"Ah. Toria."

"I was talking about my possible jobs."

"You know, you don't have to personally hold the buildings up, you just have to design them. But if Toria is as needy as she sounds, you will require your strength." She was surprised that she'd said that. Toria was none of her business—except that Julia hadn't liked how frivolous she sounded. Even though Julia had met Drew less than twenty-four hours ago, she knew he was a special person and deserved better.

He, too, looked a little taken aback by her observation. "She's a buyer for Nordstrom's," he said. "And she models on the side."

"Oh, yes. Every man's fantasy woman. You should know that she resents my chili and corn-bread casserole."

"You have a chili and corn-bread casserole?"

"I told her I'd brought one over. I had to explain my presence here somehow, and I didn't think telling her you'd helped deliver my baby was going to please her."

He grinned reluctantly. "Probably not. She's a little possessive. That's why we broke up."

"Maybe she wants to reconcile."

"Could be. I'm pretty irresistible."

She laughed and pushed the box of spring rolls toward him. "Take it. You're going to need your strength to support that ego."

The baby awoke crying. With a shrug of acceptance, Julia said, "I guess the spring roll's yours after all."

"Let me take him." He stood and scooped the baby carefully into his arms. "You can manage two minutes to eat it."

She smiled in pleased surprise. "I thought you didn't know anything about babies."

"I don't know about delivering them," he said, resuming his chair while patting the baby resting on his shoulder. "But I've acquired a little experience with children since Katherine opened the day care. A couple of times they've been down a staff member and I've been conscripted just to hold or rock a baby." He grinned as Jeremy's screech turned to a quieter whimper. "I seem to have a gift for it. Hang in there, Jeremy," he said to the baby. "Your mom's suffering from MSG deprivation."

Julia munched on the spring roll and watched him with fresh interest. "Do you want children of your own?"

"Sure. Some day," he replied.

"With Toria?"

"No. Like most of the women I've dated, she's focused on her career and not anxious to get married."

She polished off the last bite and wiped her lips and hands on a napkin. "Confirms what I've always suspected. I'm an anomaly.'' She reclaimed the baby. ''Excuse us. I'll clean this up. You go return your phone calls.''

CLETE MITCHELL WANTED to convert an old home into an office building, including an addition. He also planned to expand the small side porch into a sort of atrium where clients could wait and relax. All in all, an interesting proposition. Drew made an appointment to meet with him the following afternoon.

The Wyatts were leaving for two weeks in the Bahamas, but, according to Nadine Wyatt, who was at Cranston's office when Drew called, Drew had come highly recommended. They wanted to pay him an advance to visit the site for the music center they intended to build, and they would discuss the ideas he came us with once they returned.

''A music *center?*'' he asked, unable to believe his ears.

''Yes,'' she replied. ''It's a large piece of land. We were thinking maybe three buildings. Fountains, elegant landscaping, a pretty walkway all around the place. Something like the Music Center in L.A.''

A music center. Three buildings. He had to have misunderstood.

''I'll be happy to take a look while you're gone,'' he said in his most professional I'm-so-successful-I-don't-need-the-money tone. ''We can discuss my fee when you return.''

''Nonsense,'' Nadine Wyatt said. ''We won't take your time without seeing that you're compensated. Artists should be appreciated by each other, if not by the rest of the world. I used to be a dancer, you know.'' She named a generous amount.

Drew covered the mouthpiece to muffle his gasp.

"I'll put that in the mail today,'' she continued, "on your promise that you'll have a brilliant idea for us when we return. I'll call you then to make an appointment.''

"That'll be fine, Mrs. Wyatt.'' He thought he sounded hoarse.

She didn't seem to notice. "Thank you, Mr. Kinard.''

He hung up the phone in a mild daze. Work! The potential for lots of it. And he'd been "highly recommended.'' By his mother, probably. He'd have to ask her if she knew Nadine Wyatt. In the meantime, he'd take his praise where he could get it.

And three buildings! A very unsophisticated "Yahoo!'' perched on the tip of his tongue.

Jeanie came out of the bedroom, holding Jeremy to her shoulder and patting his back. "Was I right about the theater?''

He folded his arms. "Actually, no.''

Her face fell. "Oh. I'm sorry. I was sure…''

"They want to build a music *center*.'' He emphasized the word. "Three buildings. Fountains. Elegant landscaping.''

Her eyes brightened and a wide smile replaced her disappointed frown. "All right! That's wonderful. When are you meeting with them?''

He related the gist of their conversation.

"Wow! I know right where the site is,'' she said. "I can take you there. How wonderful, Drew.''

The sudden ding of the elevator sent him toward the small lobby. Katherine and Carmen Perez, the head teacher at Forrester Square Day Care, sidled off the elevator carrying a crib between them. Inside the crib was a car-seat/carrier combination.

Carmen was a small, dark-haired woman in her mid-fifties who had considerable experience as a kindergarten teacher. She'd also raised four boys and helped with her grandchildren.

Katherine had met her through a good friend and had actually purchased this building from Carmen. Three of her four boys had lived here, but now that they were all married, she had no use for it.

"I thought that you could use these for a few days," Katherine explained. "The carrier has a little more padding than the basket."

"Thanks, Kathy." Drew took Carmen's end of the crib in one hand while gently pushing her aside with the other. He followed Katherine as she angled the crib toward the spare bedroom.

Jeanie and Carmen paraded after them.

"Thank you, Katherine," Jeanie said. "And thank you for sending Angela to help me. She had lots of good advice."

Katherine accepted her gratitude with a nod that remained cool, despite the thoughtful gesture. "Sure. It was clever of you to find the one man in Seattle who lives over a day-care center run by his sister to help deliver your baby."

Though the remark was made playfully, there was a slightly pointed quality to it that made Drew study his sister suspiciously. But she simply smiled into his frown as they settled the crib in place beside the bed in which Jeremy had been born. She then smoothed the fabric bumper pads in place against the rails and threw back the blankets.

"I know," Jeanie replied quietly, looking directly into Katherine's eyes. "I was luckier than I deserve to be."

"I'm glad," Katherine said. "It's important to appreciate good fortune when you find it. Okay. I'm heading home. You ready, Carmen?"

Carmen stroked Jeremy's blond head and nodded. "I've been ready since eight o'clock this morning. That little Kevin Taylor is going to make an old woman of me."

Drew liked Kevin. The freckled five-year-old, who had recently moved to Seattle from Ireland, broke out of day-care routine whenever someone substituted for Carmen. He came up to visit Drew occasionally, fascinated by his drafting table and tools.

"What did he do?" Jeanie asked.

"He painted my chair," she said with a bland smile, "while I was occupied with a prospective parent. One of our younger aides was watching his group and somehow neglected to note that he was missing until she gave them snacks. He had time to do my purse, too."

Drew laughed. "He's a great kid. Too much intelligence for the company he's forced to keep."

Carmen turned to him and asked imperiously, "Are you referring to me?"

He laughed again. "I meant the other kids his age.

You, of course, are stimulating and delightful company.''

"It was a Dooney & Bourke purse," she said darkly, "that my oldest son Tomas sent from San Francisco for my birthday. It's now a very poisonous purple."

"Booney and who?" Drew asked.

"Dooney & Bourke," Jeanie corrected, emphasizing the *D*. "They make attractive and serviceable purses."

"That are very expensive," Katherine added, with a tilt of her eyebrow in Drew's direction to reinforce her earlier insistence that Jeanie was wealthy and/or privileged.

He pretended not to notice. "You should make Katherine buy you a new one," he said.

Carmen turned to Katherine with a bright smile. "What an excellent idea. And you know, the one I had was kind of small. They make a really big one with several pockets and..."

Katherine elbowed Drew as she passed him on her way to the elevator. "If you'll come with me to buy clothes for yourself, I'll buy a new purse for Carmen."

"Come on," Drew groaned. "I helped you pick out some things for Dad."

Carmen caught Drew's arm and followed Katherine. "Do it," she said in a loud whisper. "I'll make it worth your while."

He replied in the same loud whisper, "Thanks, but you're a little old for me, Carmen."

She gave him a dark look. "I was thinking of

homemade tamales. You left very little for anyone else when I brought them to our work parties.''

''Ah,'' he said, patting her hand on his arm. ''Consider it done.''

Katherine blinked. ''Honestly?''

''Honestly. I have an appointment tomorrow to talk about converting an old home into an office building, and I've been asked to prepare design ideas for a music center in Bellevue.'' He couldn't believe the thrill it gave him to say the words. Katherine's gasp of astonishment was pretty wonderful, too. As were Carmen's squeal of delight and sturdy hug.

''That's wonderful!'' Katherine stepped into his free arm with her own congratulatory embrace. ''When did this happen?''

''The call came today while we were with Dad,'' he said. ''Jeanie took the message. I returned the call. The clients—the Wyatts—are going away for a few weeks, but I'm to look over the site and have some ideas for them when they return.'' He couldn't withhold a grin. ''Three buildings.''

''Fountains,'' Jeanie added. ''Landscaping and walkways.''

''Wow,'' Katherine breathed, hugging him again. ''Have you told Mom?''

''No, I haven't,'' he admitted. ''In fact, I was wondering who was behind it. They said I came highly recommended. Sounds like Mom's work.''

''Are you talking about Bill and Nadine Wyatt?'' Katherine asked.

''Yes,'' he replied with a frown. ''You know them? Is this your work?''

She shook her head in denial. "Jordan told me he had friends looking for an architect and he'd recommended you. I didn't mention it because you know how those things go. Sometimes people remember a recommendation and sometimes they don't. Wow, Drew. The Wyatts have an international circle of friends. This could make you."

International. Now all he had to do was not choke. "Yeah, well, we shouldn't count my chickens until the designs are approved."

The elevator doors opened and Carmen shouted her congratulations again and Katherine turned to blow him a kiss before stepping inside.

When they had gone, Drew turned to find Jeanie watching him with a wistful smile. "Do you have every woman in the world wrapped around your little finger?"

"Please," he said, heading back toward the kitchen. "Katherine gives me a great deal of grief, and Carmen loves me only because her boys are now all involved in their own families and I'm someone she can cook for."

"KATHERINE ADORES YOU," Julia disputed. "And whatever grief she gives you is only because she loves you, I'm sure. Even Angela raved about you."

"She has to. She works for my sister."

"I don't think it had anything to do with that." She followed him into the kitchen. She was touched by the playful but warm exchange he'd shared with his sister and their friend, and by the sincerity of their happiness over his good news. She'd had so little sharing in her life lately. "Are you really going shopping with your sister?"

He took a carton of ice cream out of the freezer and held it up. "How do you feel about caramel ripple with chocolate-covered peanuts?"

"Deeply committed to it," she replied, going to the utensil drawer. "I'll get spoons."

He reached into a cupboard for bowls, then reached over her hands for an ice-cream scoop. She felt the brush of his fingers—strong, warm, tensile—and felt a whisper of sensation. It was just a whisper, but it was enough to startle her.

"Yes, I am going shopping." He scooped out ice cream, dropped two dollops into a bowl and handed it to her. "I generally don't waste time doing that. I get along fine from year to year on the shirts and sweaters family and friends give me for birthdays and Christmas, and replace the same jeans and cords by mail order when the old ones wear out."

"Mail order is a terrible way to shop." She dropped a spoon into his bowl of ice cream as he replaced the carton in the freezer. Then she put the sleeping baby down in his Moses basket. "You can't try things on, the pictures in the catalog often aren't even close to the color of the garment and with what it costs you for shipping and returns, you could buy another item."

When she would have sat at the table, he took the baby's basket and gestured with his bowl for her to follow him into the living room. He put the basket carefully on a simple oak coffee table, then sat on the sofa. She sat in the opposite corner. Daylight was fading, and the busy city beyond the Palladian windows quieted.

"I'd pay twice the cost of shipping," he said, "not to have to go into a store and try things on."

"But you have to try them on anyway when your catalog shipment arrives. What's the difference if you do it at home or at the store?"

"I don't try them on," he argued. "I buy the same things, so they always fit."

She rolled her eyes. "What if Carmen's tamales catch up with you one day, and the pants *don't* fit. You'll be ready to meet an important client and you won't have anything to wear because you didn't try them on first. And you'll have to return the jeans and cords and wait for another shipment to come. Meanwhile, your client finds another architect."

He shook his head. "I don't think so. I'll be internationally famous soon, according to Katherine, which means I'll be expected to be eccentric, and I can meet clients in my Joe Boxers if I want to."

She put a hand to her eyes and groaned.

He laughed. "Okay, I'll find something respectable for my meeting with the Wyatts. I suppose they wear only designer clothes?"

"She's been known to buy Oscar de la Renta's entire line for the season. I'm not sure about him."

"Is that what you do?" he asked.

The question surprised her. He asked it coolly, with no apparent purpose in mind except curiosity. But it suggested he'd noticed—or Katherine had pointed out—a few details that suggested she had money. She wondered if her Mafia family story explained that sufficiently.

Deciding she couldn't hide what he'd already surmised, she could be honest about clothing, at least.

"I've never bought a whole line," she replied, trying to be as cool as he was, "but there are a few designers I really like. And Manny loves me to be dressed to the teeth."

He nodded as though he could understand that, then met her eyes and said easily, "I thought your husband's name was Marco?"

She barely withheld a gasp. But after one single cough, she replied with a direct look into his eyes, "Marco *is* my husband. Manny is my father-in-law. The family's everything to him."

"I thought he died, and that was why Marco took over?"

Her heart slammed against her ribs, but she made herself think beyond the panic. She smiled, brazening out her second faux pas in a row. "I guess you could call moving to Florida dying, but all he's done is retire."

As soon as the words were out of her mouth, she expected him to ask, "Well, if he's living in Florida, how does he know what you're wearing?" But he didn't question her further, simply nodded and teased about having to find something suitable in his closet for his appointment tomorrow.

She went to bed early, suddenly nervous about everything. He suspected she was lying! Or had his questions just been innocently asked? Either way, with her stupid responses, it wouldn't be long before he was able to confirm his suspicions that she wasn't who she claimed to be. And if he asked her to leave, where would she take Jeremy? What would she do for a pediatrician?

She stared at her baby through the bars of the crib and wished desperately that circumstances were different.

She wondered where her uncle was right now. And whether or not he was on her trail.

And why in the heck hadn't Chloe reported in?

CHAPTER SIX

HE WAS HIRED! Drew walked home from the Queen City Grill, where he'd met Clete Mitchell, a psychologist just a few years older than he, who wanted to turn an old Victorian house into an office with a living area upstairs. Dressed in his newest jeans and wearing a shirt and tie, Drew had deferred to the warm August weather and skipped the old gray tweed sportscoat he usually wore when he wanted to look professional.

When Mitchell had met him in shorts and a Portland State University T-shirt, Drew felt himself relax. The man was quiet and watched Drew with great concentration while he talked—as though he could see the motivation behind every word and mannerism. Drew half expected him to lean across the table toward him and say, ''Your father's absent from your life, isn't he? And you've spent most of it resisting the protective cocoon your mother and sister have tried to build around you?''

Drew called himself crazy later when Mitchell listened to his ideas, watched him make a few sketches on a napkin, and declared with a sincere smile, ''Sounds as though you understand completely what I have in mind. When can I expect the plans?''

Lost in his thoughts, Drew bumped into a homeless

man standing on the corner. There were quite a few homeless in this part of Belltown. At night and in bad weather they took shelter in the underground tunnels left when the streets of Seattle were regraded after a fire in the late 1880s. The new city was partially built over the existing ground-level buildings and streets, creating a sort of catacombs.

The homeless man grumbled at Drew. Figuring he could afford to be generous after his meeting that morning, Drew gave the fellow a ten-dollar bill and wished him a great day.

The man was still staring at the bill in disbelief when Drew approached Caffeine Hy's. He glanced at his watch and saw that he was much earlier than he'd expected to be. Jeanie had told him before he left that she hoped to sleep until lunchtime today. The baby had been up a lot during the night, and when Drew had tried to help her, she'd told him firmly to go back to bed, that she had to learn to cope alone and fully intended to.

He'd found it interesting that he'd heard the baby every single time he'd awakened, and although he couldn't make out what Jeanie was saying, he could hear the gentle croon of her voice. She'd looked rough yet heroic at breakfast with the baby on her shoulder. Woman at her most giving and self-sacrificing. She'd smiled at him through her exhaustion and he'd felt a real weakness in his gut. He had to remind himself that she was lying to him.

After her curious interest in his relationship with Toria, he even wondered if there actually was a husband in the picture.

He fought hard against becoming more interested in Jeanie Shaw Abruzzo than he already was, just in case he didn't like whatever she was hiding. He had a career to get underway, and a family that was going to need him. Though he might not like the way things stood between him and Jeanie, Drew had learned a lot from his father about accepting what you couldn't change.

Not wanting to risk disturbing Jeanie, he ducked into the coffee bar for a mocha freeze.

Hyram Berg's place had just opened six months before, when Katherine bought the neighboring building. Drew's first experience there had been a simple cup of coffee bought by Katherine after she'd walked him through the future home of Forrester Square Day Care. She'd taken him to Caffeine Hy's to ask him what he thought of the building and whether or not she should buy it.

The coffee bar's décor had distracted him from the purpose of their visit. Caffeine Hy's was very Bohemian in style, and Drew liked a little less drama in his life than that. Colorful fabrics patterned in paisley, broad stripes, and other strong motifs festooned the ceiling, a beaded curtain separated the front of the shop from a storage area in the back, and the walls were painted old gold and apricot.

An oversize old sofa and mismatched chairs graced the middle of the room and a battered table at one end was surrounded by an assortment of wooden chairs. The service bar at the other end of the room was also wooden, but polished to a shine. Boxes of tea, dozens of bottles of syrup flavors, toppings and flavored sodas were lined up against a broad mirror on the wall behind it. Mounted on the wall next to that was a moose head—not the genuine work of a taxidermist, but something manufactured out of resin or plastic. It had a winking eye and a grin.

A man with his back to them had waved in the mirror as he added steamed milk to something in a tall glass, obviously for the woman in a gray wool suit who waited at the old Baroque cash register, a five-dollar bill in hand. "Hi, Katherine," he'd called to them. "I'll be right with you."

Drew had always been privately scornful of the snob-appeal popularity of coffee drinks. If he wanted caffeine, he didn't want to wait in line for it, have a lot of junk in it, or pay a fortune for it. Simple coffee satisfied his palate and kept him awake when he had work to finish. But Katherine was obviously excited about her plan and he wanted to humor her.

So he had waited in line with her while the proprietor, a nice-looking guy in his late thirties, put a lid on the paper cup, then turned and handed it to the woman. She accepted it as though she'd been given a gift. A gift that cost her four times the price of a simple cup of coffee.

When the woman left, Katherine had pulled Drew forward. "Hy, this is my brother, Drew," she said. "Drew, this is my new friend, Hyram Berg. Everybody calls him Hy. When the owner of the building showed me through the other day, my head was spinning, so I came in here to relax and think about things. Hy moved here from San Diego a couple of months ago to open this place. So he's just experienced a lot of what I'm going through.''

Hy reached across the counter to shake Drew's hand. "You're the architect?" he asked. When Drew nodded, Hy said with a gentle smile at Katherine, "She's been anxious for your opinion on the building. It's a big decision. Now, what can I get you?"

Katherine ordered a raspberry vanilla latte, then turned to Drew.

"Just coffee," he said.

"Oh, come on, Drew." She sent Hy an apologetic glance. "I know you think fancy coffee drinks are silly, but that's because you've never tried one. Live it up, okay? Try something exotic."

"But I like coffee," he'd insisted, unwilling to be charmed into falling into line with the trend. "I don't need…stuff in it."

Hy grabbed a large blue mug off a rack. "I've got a Sumatra roast you'll like," he said, proceeding to pour. He handed it across the counter. "Enjoy that. Katherine, I'll bring yours in a minute."

While Hy worked behind the counter, Katherine beckoned Drew to a small table sectioned off from the rest of the room by another beaded curtain. This must be for the buttoned-down types, Drew thought as he sat opposite her at a simple round oak table with four matching chairs. The walls were white in this corner, and nothing hung from the ceiling except a light with a simple yellow paper shade. A painting above the table boasted a female gypsy figure in a colorful costume. She was dancing barefoot in a field, a tambourine streaming ribbons uplifted in her hands.

Underneath were painted the words, *C'est toujours la fête.*

"What does that say?" he asked.

Katherine, who'd taken four years of French in high school, replied, "It's always a party. Or a celebration. Okay, listen."

She'd pulled out a notebook filled with figures and illustrations and proceeded exuberantly to carry on about all the possibilities she saw in the building and how she'd like to make them work for her.

Hy had refilled Drew's cup twice as Katherine kept talking. The next time he absconded with the cup, and when he returned with it, Drew noticed a slightly different aroma to the brew.

"This is an Americano," he explained. "Just coffee, but sort of an espresso with hot water added. The way Katherine's bending your ear, you're going to need to be sharp."

Too excited about her plan to take offense, Katherine had simply handed Hy her glass and asked for a refill.

Drew had learned two things that day. First, that his sister had researched her subject and planned carefully; if preparation counted, she was destined for success. And second, that Hy Berg made the best coffee Drew had ever tasted.

In the months since, during countless meetings at Hy's to go over floor plans and renderings for the day care, during breaks taken with Katherine's other slaves and even on his own, Drew had grown bolder. He'd experimented with chocolate, cream, and various flavors until he'd finally tried everything. He had to admit shamefacedly that his favorite drink was a mocha, and during hot weather, he'd formed an addiction to mocha freezes—a tall drink made with coffee, chocolate and ice cream. Once at closing time, Hy had added brandy.

Drew was now as much a victim of pseudo sophistication as everyone else he knew. He'd wait in line for his coffee, he loved chocolate in it and he'd pay four dollars for it. Five with a tip.

He'd since learned that Hy had lost everything, including his fiancée when his Internet price-researching company went belly-up in the dot-com disaster a couple of years earlier. He'd emerged with just enough cash to start over simply and had worked for a year as a barrista for a San Diego Starbuck's. Then he'd moved to Seattle to open his own place and apply what he'd learned.

"Mocha freeze?" Hy called out now as Drew crossed the threshold. He was bussing tables.

"Please," Drew said, taking a stool at the counter. "I can't believe I've allowed myself to be corrupted like this."

Hy laughed as he carried a plastic tub filled with cups and glasses of all sizes. "Relax. You're allowed your vulnerabilities. I used to think I had to be perfect, too. Until I lost everything." He took a tall glass off a shelf and went to work with chocolate syrup and the espresso machine. "Nothing like having to start over from scratch to give you a good perspective on what you need and what you don't."

Drew had also learned that Caffeine Hy's proprietor was as generous with philosophy as he was with his high-quality product. And he could converse on any subject.

"Anyway," Hy said, dropping a dollop of ice cream into the glass, "what's a little chocolate in your coffee going to hurt?"

Drew grinned. "It lacks dignity. Business been brisk this morning?" He indicated the full tub of cups and glasses.

"A neighborhood merchants' meeting. Millie ran her legs off, so I gave her a break." Millie Gallagher, a petite young woman who worked in the kitchen at the day care, also waited tables for Hy. "How'd your meeting with the client go?"

When Drew looked surprised that he knew, Hy explained, "Katherine was at the meeting." He fiddled with the spigots on the espresso maker and held on while it hissed and steamed. His glance took in Drew's appearance. "She was worried about what you wore to the meeting. You look okay to me."

Drew groaned as he watched Hy pour in the espresso, then blend it.

"Also heard rumors you've taken in a boarder with a baby." Hy poured the thick, creamy mixture into the glass, then added whipped cream and a chocolate-covered coffee bean on the top.

Was nothing sacred? "Katherine tell you that, too?"

"No." Hy put the drink in front of him, then leaned back against the cooler and folded his arms. "I overheard some of the staff talking about it. One of them suggested it was about time you got serious about someone, and another thought it would be nice if you got serious about *her.* I swear. Today's women have appalling taste in men.''

"Do I detect a little jealousy in that remark?" Drew dug through the whipped cream with his spoon to reach the thick coffee mixture. It was decadently delicious and still provided the caffeine jolt he needed.

Hy surprised Drew by admitting candidly, "You do." He glanced wistfully out the window as two shapely young women in shorts and tank tops walked by. "But I can't even think about women until my financial picture improves."

"Come on," Drew said. "You own a business. That's babe bait, isn't it? And this place is always filled with women. If you can't make that work for you, I wouldn't blame your single status on a lack of funds."

Hy straightened away from the cooler and threatened him with a good-natured glare as he loaded cups and glasses into the dishwasher. "Spoken like a whipper-snapper. You'd be amazed at how much works against you when money's tight. Or nonexistent."

Drew nodded apologetically. "Sorry. Didn't mean to be glib. But I'm sure there's a woman somewhere who'd love to have her own coffee supply. And the man who comes with it."

"Yeah. Until then, I'm living vicariously through my friends."

Drew laughed. "Well, try one of your other friends. This one's simply being a Good Samaritan."

Hy shook his head. "Pity."

The telephone rang and Hy excused himself to pick

it up. As he jotted down an order, Drew looked out
the window at the busy street. Pedestrians were coming and going, banners and wind socks fluttered in a
light breeze—and Jeanie was walking out of the telephone booth across the street. She looked surrepti-
tiously right, then left, and, clutching the baby to her,
hurried across the street.

She appeared anxious, and Drew wondered if
something had happened while he'd been gone. And
why was she using the pay phone when he'd noticed
a cell phone in her bag?

He went to the door to intercept her as she stepped
up onto the sidewalk.

JULIA'S HEART ROSE to her throat as she noticed Drew
standing in the doorway of the coffee bar next door
to the day care. Frowning, he stepped into her path.

"What's wrong, Jeanie?" he asked.

God, she thought, a sudden rush of emotion filling
her. *What isn't wrong? I can't stay with you forever,
my uncle's probably about to find me and I can't
reach Chloe.* What had she been thinking, agreeing
to let her friend search for the intern's body by herself? Chloe was brave and smart, but often too impulsive for her own good. What if she'd discovered
something and been found out herself? Or hurt?
Or…?

Drew's frown deepened and he caught her arm,
forcing her to focus on him.

"Are you all right?" he asked, his eyes going over
her face. He put a hand to the baby's head. Jeremy
had slept through her brief foray outside and her futile

attempts to reach Chloe at home, at work and on her cell phone. "I thought you were going to sleep in today and relax."

"I was going to," she said, hoping her smile wasn't as uncertain as her voice sounded, "but Jeremy kept waking up, so I got up and got dressed. I brought him out for some air."

He raised an eyebrow. "In the phone booth?"

He'd seen that. Of course. Drew missed nothing. "I called a friend in Vermont to see if she'd let me stay with her for a little while," she lied—again. "I didn't want to put long-distance charges on your phone." The truth was, she had a cell phone in her bag, but if her uncle was hot on her trail, calls from a cell phone could be traced.

His eyes held hers, and for a moment she thought he didn't believe her, then he said mildly, "You probably shouldn't be running around on your own if you're being chased."

She nodded. "I know. But I was only a minute."

"Yeah," he said. "But if your husband had been cruising by, that's all it would have taken."

She nodded again. "You're right."

"Come on." He pulled her toward the coffee bar. "I'll buy you the best cup of coffee you've ever had. I guess it should be decaf, but I'll bet Hy can still make something to die for. What's your pleasure?"

She forgot her problems for a moment at the prospect of an honest-to-God mocha. "A double-tall mocha, two shots, with whipped cream and chocolate jimmies."

He blinked at her. "You, too?"

"Me, too, what?"

"'Double-tall, two-shot.'" He quoted her with a mocking simper in his voice and a teasing heavenward glance. "You're a coffee nerd."

His humor dispelled her nervousness and she welcomed a return to the lightheartedness she usually felt in his company.

"I believe the term is *aficionada*," she corrected with a superior air. Then she smiled at the handsome man behind the counter. "Can you make that?"

"It would be my pleasure," he assured her.

Drew led her to a table behind a beaded curtain, then held Jeremy for her while she enjoyed her mocha. He told her about his interview, and described in detail what the client wanted to do with the house.

She loved hearing about it. She soaked up detail, watched the enthusiasm in his eyes, noticed the strong line of his jaw, the movement of his mouth as he smiled.

Suddenly she realized that she was experiencing feelings that she thought had died when Devon disappeared. While grief still remained a constant inside her, casting a shadow on every happy moment, she was becoming aware of a very real attraction to Drew Kinard. Even while she wondered how that could be, she found herself studying Drew with a new awareness.

It was only too easy to imagine his mobile mouth on hers, warm, sure, clever. She could feel herself wrapped in his embrace, her cheek against that big shoulder as his strong arms held her in place.

He'd held her once before in a less than romantic

moment when she'd been giving birth to Jeremy. She hadn't noticed the supple movements of that tall body then, just the solidity of the arms wrapped around her, the rocklike chest she'd leaned back against for the final push.

Maybe that was it, she thought. He represented safety and security for herself and her child—at least for the moment—and some primitive instinct drew her to him, made her want him.

She saw that he was aware of her sharpened attention on him. As he smiled a question at her, she noticed the easy tenderness that seemed so at odds with all that muscle. Her baby was cuddled against his chest, Drew's large hand holding him in place. *God!* she thought with a panicky desperation. *I feel like I'm falling in love!* But how could that be? She'd known him for barely two days. Dr. Jessup was right—her hormones must be completely out of whack.

"You look as though you're terrified of me one minute," he said, the questioning smile turning to concern, "and as if I'm your long-lost lover the next. What are you thinking?"

She took her last sip of mocha and pushed the cup away, unwilling to lie to him any more than she already had. But she tried to express her confusing emotions with casual savvy so that she didn't scare him to death.

"You're absolutely right," she said as she pushed her chair back. "I was just thinking how lucky I am that the fates led me to your door Sunday evening, but how scary it is to have feelings for someone again."

As she leaned over him to take the baby from him, their eyes locked. She swore she heard the click. She couldn't straighten.

"You have feelings for me?" he asked.

All attempts to be casual or savvy fled. Her hand, caught between her baby and his chest, felt his heart-beat—strong, steady, slightly accelerated.

"Yes," she admitted in a whisper. "But I might just be...confusing them for...something else."

"You mean gratitude," he said.

She should have left it at that. It would have been an easy, believable truth, because gratitude was a very strong part of what she felt for him.

But it wasn't the biggest part. Something else she couldn't quite define seemed to be filling her with... what? Possibilities? An odd hopefulness that had been absent from her life for months now was making her think that there might be a future for her out there somewhere.

And it was more than her beautiful baby that made her look ahead. It was Drew. She hadn't had dreams in so long, but suddenly she was imagining the three of them in a house of his own design on the Sound. How could this be, she thought frantically, when she'd just finally learned that Devon was gone?

In truth, though, he'd been lost to her since he'd disappeared. She and Chloe had tried to support each other's hopes, but she'd known deep inside that she'd never see him again. Love, she guessed, knew when its soul was gone.

But Devon's spirit remained with her, and his strong belief that truth and justice were everything.

She couldn't help wondering what he'd think of her now for the way she'd lied to Drew.

And that somehow prevented her from lying about how she felt.

"No," she said quietly. "Not gratitude."

His free hand went to her cheek and his dark eyes focused on her mouth. She felt herself lean closer, eager to finally know what his mouth felt like on hers.

Then she remembered that according to her lie, she was supposed to be married.

She straightened abruptly, then took the baby from him. "I'm sorry," she whispered. "I...I..."

"I understand." He drew a breath, then he stood, too, his expression unreadable, and led her out the door with a wave in Hy's direction.

Hy, who'd probably seen that almost-encounter, watched them with a concerned smile as they left the coffee bar.

Julia's heart was thumping. She was torn between wanting to explore a relationship with Drew and accepting that she had no right to explore anything with anyone until she'd proved her uncle a murderer and put him behind bars. Only then could she ensure that she and her baby and whoever shared in their life were safe.

But if she didn't tell him the truth soon, it would be too late to save whatever they might have together.

She mistrusted people who had no moral compass. There was always a right and a wrong thing to do. At least, that was what she'd thought. But in this case, while it would be right to tell the truth, it would be wrong to expose her baby to the dangers they might encounter if Drew told her to leave.

Still, she doubted seriously that he would. Though only twenty-six, he had the kind of maturity that usually came with age. He was kind and protective and responsible. And he didn't mind diapering a baby. What woman wouldn't love him?

So there it was—morally, she was waffling. But the unfortunate truth was that she didn't give a rip. She could tell him the truth without danger of eviction, but it might destroy the bond developing among the three of them. She wasn't risking it.

CHAPTER SEVEN

"PLEASE DON'T LOOK like that," Drew said as he led her into the elevator and pushed the button. Beyond the day-care doors, he could hear Carmen's voice singing about bees and flowers, then the children's voices repeating after her.

At least there were no birds involved. He didn't want to think about birds and bees right now. Though he occasionally went for long stretches without a woman in his bed, he'd seldom felt as frustrated as he did at this moment. And all because of a woman who had a husband, who was in danger, who'd just had a baby and couldn't assuage his frustration for weeks, even if she wanted to.

Great. At least his work was going well.

"Look like what?" she asked in surprise.

"Like there's no solution and you're going to have to run forever," he replied. "That doesn't have to be the case if you take steps to change things." He sounded cranky. That was all right because he felt cranky.

"I know that," she replied a little defensively. "And I'm going to. I just want to feel a little stronger before I have to deal with an attorney and the police and probably…Marco."

Was it his imagination or was she now having difficulty remembering the characters in her little drama?

"You're sure you can trust your friend?" he asked as the elevator ascended.

"What friend?"

"The friend in Vermont," he replied. "The one you just risked life and limb to call from the phone booth."

There was a spark of temper in her wide blue eyes and she withdrew from him several paces. Apparently she didn't like his tone. "Yes, I can trust her," she said. "And I explained why I went to the phone booth."

"Well, next time," he said, "I'd rather you put a charge on my phone bill than risk your life and Jeremy's."

"Really," she replied coolly. "Because you sound as though you wouldn't mind at all if I was bumped off."

He gave her the look that comment deserved. "That doesn't even warrant an answer."

"Well, that's a relief," she grumbled.

When the elevator door opened on the third floor, Drew held it back while Jeanie stepped out with the baby. Almost immediately she stopped still.

"Who's that?" she asked.

Certain her question meant they had an intruder, possibly someone sent by her husband, he yanked her back into the elevator and stepped out in front of her—only to find that they were facing danger all right, but of quite another sort.

Kevin Taylor, escape artist extraordinaire, stood

outside Drew's door. The green-eyed five-year-old with curly red-brown hair was the bane of Katherine's existence. He was smart and cute and there wasn't a locked door in the building that could hold him.

"This is the famous Kevin Taylor," Drew said, stepping out to lift the boy onto his hip. "Kevin, this is my *friend* Jeanie." He grinned over the word, in light of their recent argument.

Jeanie responded with a wry glance, then turned her attention to the boy. "Hi, Kevin."

"Where'd you get the baby?" Kevin asked in his lilting Irish accent.

"He's my little boy."

"Is he coming to the day care?"

"No. I'm just visiting with Drew for a while."

Kevin patted Drew's shoulder. "Drew's my buddy. I came to visit, too. Where you been?"

Drew turned toward the apartment, his key in hand. "I had work to do," he said patiently. "And I appreciate that you like to visit me, Kevin, but we talked about this the last time you came up, remember? You can't just walk away from Carmen when you feel like it. You have to stay in class so that someone knows where you are all the time and that you're safe."

"But *you* know where I am."

"That's true, but I don't work for the day care."

Kevin wrinkled his nose as Drew unlocked the door. "You don't? How come? You live here."

"Yes, but I just rent this apartment from my sister."

"That's Katherine."

"Right." Drew went directly to the telephone and

called Katherine. He could hear a commotion behind her. "Kevin's up here," he said. "I'll bring him right down."

He heard her groan. "Carmen figured as much. She's already on her way up. Sorry about that."

"It's not a problem for me," he said, "but you're going to have to do something about it before it becomes a problem for you."

"Thanks for pointing that out." Her reply was sharp. "I didn't think anyone would mind if I lost a child or two."

"Kathy..." he began.

"Yes, Andrew?" she countered.

When they were down to the names only their mother was allowed to call them, he knew there was nothing to be gained in the conversation.

"I love you," he said, grinning at the knowledge that that would defuse her annoyance.

"I love you, too, you big dweeb." She hung up the phone.

He turned to find Jeanie leading Carmen into the apartment. Carmen was stone-faced, her color high.

"Oh-oh," Kevin said, holding more tightly to him.

Carmen stopped before them, her hands on her hips. Drew saw her take a deep breath and close her eyes, as though collecting herself.

"Kevin," she said finally, opening her eyes and looking sternly at the boy, "you cannot just walk out of the room and wander off when you feel like it. We were all very worried about you."

Kevin sighed. "The song was boring, and Drew

has that funny slanty desk and all those colored pencils.''

"But Drew is working on that drafting board with all those colored pencils. And it isn't nice to bother him.''

Kevin leaned out of Drew's arms toward Jeanie. "He makes drawings,'' he told her importantly, "so that the carpenter guys know how to make a building.''

Jeanie nodded. "Yes, I knew that.''

"Come on, Kevin.'' Carmen took the boy from Drew, then set him on his feet. She held him firmly by the hand. "Tell Drew thank-you for his hospitality.''

Kevin clearly wanted more information. "What's that?''

"It's for letting you visit.''

"But he didn't. He called Katherine.''

"Then apologize for bothering him.''

"I didn't. He wasn't even here.''

Carmen rolled her eyes while Drew struggled to maintain a straight face.

"Can't I just say goodbye?'' Kevin asked.

"By all means.''

Kevin offered Drew his free hand. "Goodbye. Someday, can I come and see you when you don't have to send me back?''

Drew squatted down to look into the boy's disappointed face and shake his hand. He didn't know Kevin's situation, just that his father was a nice guy with a very successful computer company, and apparently a single father. Kevin seemed happy and well-adjusted, but more advanced than his contemporaries.

"Maybe one day your dad will bring you over so that you can use the drafting table," he suggested.

"That'd be cool!"

"But we have to ask first."

"Today?"

"Not today. But as soon as I can."

"Okay."

Drew saw them onto the elevator, then returned to his apartment to find Jeanie in the bedroom with the door closed. That meant she was feeding Jeremy.

He went to work in his office, noting and sketching some ideas he'd had for the old house on the walk home. When he emerged some time later, feeling hungry, Jeanie was in the kitchen making sandwiches.

He liked walking into the kitchen and seeing her there, the baby on a chair in the carrier Katherine had brought last night. She turned to give him a quick smile. "I was getting hungry," she said. "Hope you don't mind."

"Of course not. You're welcome to whatever you want."

THAT WAS AN INTERESTING NOTION, Julia thought, considering just what it was she was beginning to want.

"I was thinking I should get serious about leaving," she said, slicing sandwiches in half at an angle. She was going to be grateful and polite so there wouldn't be a repeat of their argument in the elevator.

She'd hate it if they parted company angry with each other.

"Leaving me or your...husband?" he asked, reaching over her head for glasses.

Annoyance flared in her and she turned to him, ready to tell him to back off. So much for her gratitude. But he was so close that all kinds of emotions and reactions defused her anger—like her palpitations at the nearness of his strong, broad shoulders, the long fingers reaching for the glasses.

"Leaving here," she corrected breathlessly. Some strange, out-of-sync instinct reminded her of how much she'd loved Devon. Then another told her that this feeling she had for Drew also deserved life. But she was so torn. Leaving really was a good idea.

Drew went to the refrigerator for a carton of milk, and she took a steadying breath. She carried the sandwich plates to the table while he poured the milk. "To go to Vermont?"

"I don't know."

"You should have a plan before you start moving around."

He carried their glasses to the table. She sat in her usual place and tried to change the subject.

"Have you come up with any more ideas for Dr. Mitchell's place?" she asked pleasantly.

"Not yet," he replied, then changed the subject back. "I thought you wanted to let the baby adjust a little, to gain strength yourself before moving on."

She hesitated, striving for patience. He was the kind of man you had to hit with a brick!

"We're complicating your life," she said. "And you're not doing mine much good, either."

"My life's always been complicated," he retorted. "And you're the one messing up your life, not me."

She didn't want to take part in another conversation where she had to lie. "Drew, I don't want to talk about it. Can we just enjoy our lunch?"

"If you promise not to do anything foolish."

More foolish than moving in with a stranger and lying to him about having a husband?

"I promise."

"Then, let's eat."

THE NEXT COUPLE OF DAYS PASSED in wonderful slow motion. Jeremy thrived, Julia felt physically stronger, and life in the apartment above Forrester Square Day Care took on a cozily domestic pattern.

Drew fixed breakfast while Julia fed Jeremy, they ate together, then Drew went to his office at the other end of the apartment and worked on the project for Mitchell.

Julie tidied, did laundry, played with the baby, who was beginning to respond to the sound of her voice, and to Drew's. Drew had even taken turns holding the baby after his night feedings so Julia could get some sleep.

One day they'd driven in Drew's truck to the Wyatts' property, with Julia navigating, and spent an hour, walking from one end of the site to the other. Drew had taken photographs and made notes. He ordered a geological study, and while he waited for it, he continued work on the Mitchell project.

Most days Julia prepared lunch and he cleaned up. While the baby was awake, she spent time talking to him, playing music, telling him stories.

On the nights Drew got up with him, Julia heard him talk to the baby conversationally about cars and tools and women. If any one thing about him made her feelings for him grow, it was the time he was willing to give Jeremy.

"You have to hear this stuff from someone," his mellow voice murmured one night. The windows were open and the fresh salt smell of the ocean filled the quiet apartment. "Your mom will tell you about food and clothes and good manners, and that's great, but the other guys are going to laugh at you if that's all you know. Take it from me. I grew up with a mother and a sister, and I was always in trouble with the other guys. A piece of advice. If you know what a sifter is, don't share that knowledge with your friends. They won't appreciate it. Or you."

Julia had smiled to herself and gone back to sleep, secure in the knowledge that Drew knew what he was doing—with the baby and with his life.

She just wished the same could be said for her.

The one bleak spot in those wonderful days was that she still hadn't heard from Chloe. If she didn't hear soon, she might have to risk her own safety and go to the police. She hadn't wanted to until she had a solid case so the police could charge her uncle before he escaped or exacted revenge on her.

She decided to give it one more day. If she still hadn't heard from Chloe, she would tell Drew the truth and go to the police.

JULIA ANSWERED the doorbell on Friday morning to find Katherine standing there in a white sundress, a straw bag slung over her shoulder.

"Hi!" Julia greeted her warmly, stepping aside. "Come in."

Katherine's return smile held its usual reservation. Julia wished things were different, but she couldn't expect Katherine to understand her situation, and she wasn't in a position to explain it.

"I was wondering if Drew was available to go shopping," Katherine asked. "I've got lots of help today, and I thought we could spend the morning at the mall."

Drew had wandered out of his office and said regretfully, "I'm sorry, Katherine. I have an appointment with a client today."

"No, you don't," Julia corrected cheerily.

His gaze was threatening. "I have to prepare for a meeting with…"

"No, you don't," she repeated, grinning in the face of his displeasure. "You promised Carmen. If you don't go shopping with Katherine, Carmen doesn't get her purse." She frowned at the jeans and chambray shirt that were his uniform. "And you really need some clothes."

He looked from her to his sister and sighed defeatedly. "You're not going to make me buy anything I don't want," he warned.

Katherine agreed with a single nod. "I wouldn't think of it."

"And Jeanie and Jeremy are coming with us," he insisted.

Julia was thrilled at the prospect, even if he intended the invitation punitively. Shopping! How normal and wonderful a thing to do after the week she'd endured. And she figured the risk of running into her uncle or one of his men was slim. Besides, she really needed to buy more sleepers and diapers for Jeremy. But her pleasure wavered as she turned to Katherine, expecting her to object, or at least be less than enthusiastic.

To her surprise, Katherine shooed them toward the bedrooms. "Then hurry up before a crisis develops downstairs and I lose my window of opportunity. I'll sit at the kitchen table with the newspaper."

As Drew shuffled off to his room, Julia ran excitedly to hers. Still in her bag was a soft, pink knit outfit she'd bought months ago in anticipation of the week following delivery. When she'd packed in a hurry Sunday afternoon, it had been in the front of her closet, still in its plastic sleeve, so she'd grabbed it.

She shook it out now, wishing she'd hung it up days ago. At the bottom of her bag was a small purse she hadn't had occasion to use yet. When she and Chloe had stopped at the bank at Pike Place Market, she'd stuffed a considerable amount of cash in it, knowing she'd need the reserves for hotel living.

Now she pulled wads of bills out of it to make room for lipstick and a comb, leaving enough cash for shopping. Then she remembered she'd need diapers, wipes and a hat for Jeremy.

Jeremy! She'd left him on the kitchen table in his carrier while she cleaned up the breakfast dishes.

He'd been asleep, but she was afraid a baby, even a sleeping one, would be the last thing Katherine would want to deal with on her morning off.

Dressed in her new outfit, Julia hurried into the kitchen to find Katherine holding Jeremy's tiny hand, the paper forgotten as she watched him sleep.

"Want me to move him?" Julia asked, feeling like an intruder.

"No," Katherine replied with a smile over her shoulder. "But see if you can get Drew moving, will you?" The smile was genuine and without its usual restraint. The baby, Julia knew, had softened her opposition to their company on the shopping trip.

She headed back to her room to retrieve her purse and the diapers and wipes. Then she turned, ready to rap on Drew's door and hurry him along as she'd promised Katherine.

But he was already there, standing in *her* doorway.

Her heart sank to her toes as she became aware of two things simultaneously. First, she'd left twenty and fifty-dollar bills strewn all over the bed in careless piles. Even a cursory glance would have shown the total to be considerable—minus the few hundred she'd put back into her purse.

Secondly, though Drew now had his back to the bed and was gesturing her to be quick, he'd had plenty of time to see the money. In fact, she didn't know how he could have missed it.

But all he asked was, "Are you ready? Katherine's going to blame me for holding things up, you know."

So. He was going to pretend he hadn't seen it.

She didn't know why, but she couldn't let him get

away with that. It would have been easier. All part of the lie. But she couldn't.

She angled her chin at him. "Don't you want to ask about the money?"

He shook his head. "I just figured you helped your husband clean out one of his Vegas slot machines before you decided to leave him." That smart response delivered, he pointed toward the kitchen. "I'll get the baby."

DREW TOOK A CERTAIN SATISFACTION in leaving Jeanie standing there with her mouth open. He lingered in the doorway an extra moment, hoping she'd come clean, but she didn't. She simply stared.

So he got the baby and his sister and held the elevator until Jeanie came bustling after them, a small purse over her shoulder, a clutch of diapers and a plastic jar of wipes in her hand.

"We have to get you a diaper bag," Katherine said as she pressed the down button.

Once they reached Katherine's car, Drew installed the carrier in the back seat. While the women talked, he wondered if there was anything to Katherine's suggestion that Jeanie was running from the law. But he dismissed the thought immediately. She seemed so polished and gentle. Of course, she had lied to him. But, then, there'd been nothing secretive about all that cash strewn around. Maybe it *was* hers.

It took both women to help extricate him from the back seat once the carrier was in place. Then Julia sat next to the baby and he got in the front beside Kath-

erine. There wasn't much more leg room, but at least
he didn't feel that he was eating his knees.

"God, I'll be glad when you get a decent-size car,"
he grumbled as Katherine drove off.

She shook her head at the road. They had this discussion regularly. "It's a classic and I love it. Quit
complaining."

Shopping with his sister and Jeanie wasn't quite
the misery Drew had expected it to be. The clerk,
mercifully, was a man and seemed to perceive instantly what he was up against—bullying from Katherine, passive-aggressive suggestions from Jeanie.

The clerk extended his hand to Drew. "I'm Horace," he said.

Drew wasn't surprised by the antiquated name. The
man was short and spindly and looked as if he belonged in a Dickens novel, though he was nattily
dressed in a three-piece suit. He surveyed Drew with
a practiced eye.

"Your preferred style is casual," he pronounced.

Drew turned to Katherine with a superior look.

She sighed and shook her head. "Don't get cocky.
That's a polite way of saying grungy."

"Drew's just more cerebral than fashion-con-
scious," Jeanie said bracingly.

Katherine criticized her support of him with raised
brows, then took the baby from her. "I'm not going
to be able to stand this. I got him here—you're responsible for getting him out with several changes of
clothes aimed at convincing his clients that he's an
architect, not a hovel builder. I'll go find you a diaper
bag." And she strode away with Jeremy in the carrier.

Jeanie turned to the clerk. "You have to make me look good, Horace."

Horace smiled. "Leave it to me."

Drew and Horace conferred over pants while Jeanie hovered nearby, offering an occasional suggestion. Drew refused to encourage her, but Horace seemed to think she had a point when she suggested that pleated fronts were dressier than the flat front Drew preferred.

She grinned at him. "And remember that this is going to earn you Carmen's tamales. If you gain five pounds, you don't want them to show."

Horace put a pair of charcoal and a pair of khaki pants over Drew's arm, then led the way to shirts and sweaters. He picked out a couple of plaid cotton shirts, several sweaters, and a flannel shirt in a wine color.

Jeanie suggested the indigo instead.

Horace frowned. "But merlot's the color for fall."

Jeanie held the blue shirt up to Drew's face. "But blue's his color."

Horace apparently concurred and put the wine shirt back.

Drew was pleasantly surprised to learn that he had a color—and that Jeanie had noticed.

She wandered toward a rack of sports jackets and chose a brown wool with suede elbow patches. "What do you think of this?" she asked. "You'd look dressy without feeling too formal." She also held up a corduroy in a similar color. "Or this?"

"I'll try the wool one," he conceded.

"It'd look good with jeans, too. What do you think, Horace?"

"Absolutely." The clerk went to a wall filled with cubbyholes of jeans.

"Thirty-six, thirty-six," Drew called after him. But he felt sure Horace already knew that.

ONCE AGAIN, Julia had to admit to ambivalence. She was here to assist Drew in buying clothes to help him make a good impression with his clients, not to enjoy the sight of his tight backside as he emerged from the fitting room and evaluated the different combinations in the department's three-way mirror.

But she had to take advantage of the opportunity.

The look she liked best, she thought with an upsurge of affection as Drew executed a comical runway spin that made even Horace laugh, was the jeans with the indigo shirt and the brown jacket. It was so Drew—casual and masculine, with an easy elegance he seemed completely unaware he possessed.

Horace suggested a few turtlenecks to go with the jacket—an inspired idea. Then Drew spotted a black leather flight jacket. He tried it on, but decided to put it back because of the price tag.

While he was busy with Horace, picking out socks, she took the jacket to another clerk and bought it for Drew. Horace was just finishing packing up Drew's purchases when Katherine returned with the baby and her own bags. Julia reclaimed Jeremy, and in the shuffle of bags, she was sure Drew never noticed the extra one.

They stopped at a Starbuck's in the mall for coffee,

choosing a quiet corner booth so Julia could feed the baby in privacy. While Jeremy nursed, Drew and Katherine lapsed into conversation about the day care.

"I wish Dad could be here for our opening," Katherine said, stirring cream into her latte with a straw.

"All those people would probably make him uncomfortable." Drew snapped off the end of her biscotti and dunked it in his cappuccino. "I'm sure he'd prefer a personal, Katherine-conducted tour at a quieter time." He popped the bite of cookie into his mouth.

She nodded, a frown still pleating her forehead.

"What?" Drew asked, teasing her with a grin. "You're not supposed to be thinking about anything but style today. How can I trust you to help me buy shoes if your mind's elsewhere?"

She took a sip of her drink, then leaned her chin in her palm. "Alexandra turned down our invitation again," she said. "Hannah got on the phone with me. We told her how well the day care was going so far, how much we could use her expertise in business management and how much she'd love the kids." She sighed. "But she still won't come."

Hannah, Julia knew, was Katherine's partner in the day care. She did the accounting. Their fathers had been business partners, and the children had remained friends. Apparently Alexandra was the daughter of Drew's father's third partner.

Suddenly aware that Julia was left out of the conversation, Katherine turned to her with an apologetic smile. "I'm sorry, Jeanie. That was rude. Alexandra Webber is an old friend of Drew's and Hannah's and mine. She went to live with family in Montana when her parents died, but since she graduated she's been a bit of a rolling stone. Hannah and I have been trying to encourage her to come back to Seattle and join us in the business.''

"Maybe she's happy where she is," Drew suggested.

Katherine fixed him with her frown. "I told you when Hannah and I came back from visiting her last time that she looks great but she has these nightmares about the fire. One night I was sleeping in the room right next door to hers and she about scared me to death when she woke up screaming.''

"You said she was seeing a doctor about them."

"Yes, but I'm not sure I believe her. I think it'd be good for her to come back here and face the place where it all happened. It might help her get those images out of her mind so she can lead a more normal life. She seems so...I don't know. Lost, I guess.''

Drew stole another bite of her biscotti. "And what qualifies you to know what's best for her, Ms. Freud?''

His sister rolled her eyes at him. "Friendship. Love. The desire to reestablish the Forrester Square Triumvirate! We were all so good for each other once, even though we were just kids. I think we could be good together again.''

"All I remember is how the three of you used to persecute me," Drew said wryly.

"And deservedly so." Katherine picked up what was left of her cookie. "You were such a little pill.''

When Jeremy was finished, Julia tugged down her

shirt and put him over her shoulder to pat his back. "Maybe she'd come just to visit," she suggested quietly. "Not to see the old haunts, or think about becoming part of the business. She might be afraid you'll want to relive the past together, and she doesn't feel up to doing that. But just being with old friends would be nonthreatening. You could go camping or hiking, or something you didn't do as children."

Katherine turned to her, frown still in place, and for a moment Julia thought she'd overstepped. Then Drew's sister raised an eyebrow. "That's a thought," she said, then added with only a hint of reluctance, "Thank you."

Jeremy burped, punctuating their discussion.

Reaching into one of her shopping bags, Katherine pulled out a blue diaper bag and handed it to Julia. The fabric was decorated with white bunnies and yellow ducklings. Katherine opened it to show the mesh pockets in which she'd already installed the diapers and wipes. There were more pockets for bottles and all the other things babies needed.

"Gaudy, but don't you love it?" She pushed Julia's hand away when she reached for her purse. "No, don't pay me. It's a gift."

"Thank you," Julia said, looking to Drew for an explanation of his sister's generosity.

"She likes to play with your head," he whispered as they gathered up their packages.

Julia thought the search for shoes might be grisly, but Drew settled almost immediately on a pair of casual midcut boots that Katherine held up for his inspection. They were dark brown with dark stitching.

She ran a finger along the top of the opening. "A padded collar for comfort." She took his index finger and made him touch the inside. "Cushioned insole." She ran her finger along the stitching. "And a sturdy look that could go from hiking trail to office—as long as you remember to polish them. What do you think?"

He bought them, and the same pair in a lighter honey color.

Katherine put an arm around Julia's shoulders as he paid, and Julia became hopeful that things were changing between them. "That was easier than I anticipated," Katherine confided.

"I know!"

"Now comes the hard part."

"What's that?"

"I think you should get a haircut," Katherine said to Drew as he rejoined them. Before he could protest, she added quickly, "I know your hair isn't your fault, but I think one of those shorter styles trimmed close in the back but allowed to be messy in the front would lend itself to your particular…" She struggled over the right word.

"Casual chic," Julia added helpfully.

Katherine smiled at her, laughter in her eyes. "That's a kind way of putting it."

"If you two are going to be rude," he threatened gravely, "Jeremy and I are going golfing." He took the carrier from Julia and headed out of the shoe store.

Julia and Katherine followed, relieved when he turned into a barbershop at the very end of the mall. Directly across from it was a Dooney & Bourke store.

Katherine left Julia seated on a bench near a fenced-off square filled with plants and went to buy Carmen's purse.

Surrounded by their packages, Julia watched Drew through the big window. As the barber greeted him, he took Jeremy from his carrier and pointed out into the mall at Julia. He ran a hand over his hair, as though explaining what he wanted.

The barber nodded in obvious agreement and encouraged him into a chair, draping a cape loosely over his shoulders. Drew held Jeremy against him, and the barber gave him a small towel to protect the baby's face.

As the barber went to work, Drew chatted with him, absently stroking Jeremy, his big hand almost covering her baby from head to toe.

Julia felt as though her heart might burst. She was in love, she realized with complete conviction. Even with love for Devon still alive in her, and grief at his loss, she'd been given this…unexpected blessing. She didn't know how else to describe it.

When Drew came out of the barbershop, he looked absolutely gorgeous. The back and sides of his hair had been closely trimmed, but the top, left a little longer, looked fashionably disheveled and totally appealing. It seemed to define the angles of his face and dramatize his eyes.

Even Katherine, just arriving with Carmen's purse, stared at him openmouthed. "Drew!" she breathed. "You're…really…"

Again, she groped for the right word.

"Hunky," Julia supplied. Then, needing to distract

herself from how deeply in love she'd fallen at the absolutely worst possible time in her life, she said urgently, "I'm starved. Can we have lunch?"

An hour and a half later, Katherine had gone back to work, and Drew had headed into his office to return phone calls.

Julia placed a sleeping Jeremy in his crib and left her own purchases on the chair. As she passed Drew's half-opened door, she noticed that all his bags lay in a heap on the bed. Hurrying inside, she found the black leather jacket and hung it up at the back of his closet.

"I CAN'T BELIEVE you helped a woman give birth to a baby and didn't tell me," Drew's mother scolded him over the phone that afternoon.

"Mom, I'm just getting used to the idea myself," Drew explained. "Jeanie was just a woman in trouble and I tried to help."

"Katherine tells me she claims her husband's a *mafioso*."

"You say that as though you grew up in 'The Family,'" he teased. "And yes, she does."

"But we don't believe her?"

We. He smiled to himself. His mother supported everything he and Katherine did. If they didn't believe Jeanie's story, then neither did she. Even if she'd never met Jeanie.

"Right," he said.

"Katherine thinks she's trouble."

"I think she's *in* trouble."

"Mmm." His mother sounded as though she

agreed, and for a moment he thought he was going to get off easy. Then she added abruptly, "I want to meet her."

"Mom…"

"You're coming for dinner tomorrow night."

"Mom…"

"Six-thirty."

And that was that. A royal proclamation.

Jeanie looked worried the following day as they prepared to leave. She had Jeremy dressed in a new blue jumpsuit with giraffes on it, and had put on the long flowered skirt and silky pink blouse she'd bought after lunch yesterday. She was brushing her hair and wandered familiarly in and out of his room as he put on his second shoe and sock.

"She wants to tell you I'm no good for you," she speculated. "Did you assure her there's nothing going on? Did you explain that we're not…? That I'm…?"

He was feeling cranky again. All the women in his life seemed to believe it was their job to tell him what he was thinking and feeling. It was time for him to set them straight.

"There *is* something going on," he corrected her firmly, "even though we can't act on it. And we would be lovers if you hadn't just had a baby and if…" *And if you weren't lying to me.*

She had brushed her hair into one hand and was about to wrap a band around it. At his words, she gasped, and her hair fell loose, raining around her face in a soft, golden shower. He had to concentrate on putting on his shoe.

"You told her that?" she demanded.

He shook his head. "No, but she's a smart woman and she and Katherine talk all the time."

Jeanie remained across the room, fidgeting with the covered elastic in her fingers. She watched warily as Drew went to the closet for one of his new turtlenecks. The evening forecast was cool.

"All that about being lovers…" she began. The word *lovers* seem to reverberate in the room.

"You want to deny it?" He pulled the sweater on over his head. When he emerged, he saw that she'd folded her arms over her chest and her blue gaze was direct.

"No," she said. "But I don't think it would be wise to tell your mother that."

"I wouldn't," he assured her. "But she reads me pretty well."

Jeanie opened her mouth to speak, then shook her head against whatever she'd intended to say and walked out of the room.

"Is Katherine going to be there?" she shouted back at him.

"No," he replied. "Just us."

"We should pick up a bunch of flowers."

Drew heard that suggestion as he reached into the closet for a belt on his wall rack and noticed something black and unfamiliar on a hanger. He pulled out the leather flight jacket he'd looked at in the store yesterday.

For several seconds he was confused, then the identity of his benefactor came to him. He didn't know whether he felt pleased or annoyed.

"Jeanie!" he bellowed.

There was a moment's hesitation, then she replied warily, "Yeah?"

"Come here!"

"I'm busy!"

He found her in the kitchen, putting diapers into her new bag.

"What's this?" he demanded, holding up his discovery.

She glanced up at him with an innocent smile. "I believe it's called a jacket. Bomber style."

He scolded her smart reply with a look. "Why is it in my closet?"

"Because you, slovenly individual that you are, left it in the middle of your bed."

He took the distracting diaper bag out of her hands and put it aside. "It was almost three hundred dollars."

"Two hundred and thirty-nine is not almost..."

"That's not the point!" he interrupted a little loudly.

She waited a moment. "What is the point?" she asked quietly.

He knew she wanted him to ask her about the money on the bed. And he wanted her to trust him enough to explain it without his having to ask.

"I don't know," he said finally, lowering his voice. "I guess I'm not in the habit of receiving gifts from women."

"Then you'll have to stop rescuing pregnant women on your doorstep, and providing shelter and chocolate-covered Oreos." She smiled and put her hand to his arm in a conciliatory gesture. "It was a simple thank-you, not a challenge to your masculinity.''

He felt that touch to the very core of his being. But not quite sure where he stood, he simply nodded. ''Then you're welcome. Next time, just the words will do.''

DREW COULD SEE almost instantly that Jeanie made a good impression on his mother. Helen Kinard was an old-fashioned woman with a spine of steel but a style that was all good manners, gentle words, and graceful behavior.

Jeanie, Drew was beginning to discover, displayed all those things when not delivering a baby or butting heads with him. She greeted his mother with warmth and charm, then handed her the baby, who won her heart by staring up at her with his slightly unfocused gaze.

They walked into the living room of the modest but nicely appointed three-bedroom Craftsman Drew's family had moved into after selling the Forrester Square place in the Queen Anne district. His mother had repainted a few years earlier, and Drew had just finished adding a deck and a greenhouse as a surprise for his father's homecoming.

''What a lovely lamp,'' Jeanie said, going to his mother's favorite piece in the room. ''It's Cheuret, isn't it?'' The bronze lamp with the alabaster tulip-shaped shades had been in their home for as long as Drew could remember.

His mother, still holding the baby, studied her a moment in surprise, then replied, ''It is. Lou bought it for me on our honeymoon. Not many people know what it is. Everyone's a Tiffany snob, it seems.''

''My mother had one with a double shade,'' Jeanie explained. ''I'm not sure what happened to it when she died.''

Katherine had apparently neglected to mention that Jeanie's parents were no longer living. ''I'm sorry,'' Helen said.

Jeanie straightened. ''Thank you. She and my father died together in a train wreck. I was eleven, so I've had a lot of time to adjust. Want me to take Jeremy? It's amazing how heavy a baby can become—even a little guy like mine.''

''I know.'' Helen inclined her head toward Drew. ''This one came into the world weighing ten pounds. I didn't get any sleep until he was three. Is Jeremy sleeping much?''

Drew watched them walk together toward the conservatory and felt a clutch of emotion. He had a sudden image of the two of them and Katherine preparing Thanksgiving dinner while he and his father and Jeremy and Carlos, Katherine's foster son, watched football. The picture was so beautiful that he indulged himself for a moment.

When he came back to reality, Jeanie was standing in the middle of the conservatory, turning in a small circle as she studied the plants hanging from the domed ceiling, standing on the stone floor, and displayed on small decorative tables and plant stands. A wrought-iron settee and chair covered in red-and-yellow-flowered cushions sat in a corner.

''I'd love a room just like this,'' she said.

Drew was certain Jeanie had no idea that her words sounded as though she wanted him to build one for her, leaving his mother with the impression that they were planning a future together.

His mother turned to him, her expression complex. He could tell she liked Jeanie. A lot. But she was still concerned for Drew.

"I see you've bought some new plants," he observed, putting his arm around her. He pointed to a tall pink flower questioningly.

"Astilbe. Your father always loved them. He's going to enjoy this room."

Drew nodded. "I hope so." His father's only complaint while in prison had been the lack of sunlight and the fact he couldn't see the sky except for an hour every day in the exercise yard. The Seattle area wasn't the sunniest of places, but the glass-enclosed room would allow him to stare at the sky all day long.

A bell rang in the kitchen and his mother excused herself to see to dinner.

"I'd never leave a room like this," Jeanie said, putting a fingertip to a purple-blue hydrangea. "Having a mocha in this room with the baby in my arms would be perfection—no, wait."

"Something missing?"

She pointed to a corner bare of plants and flowers. "I'd put a torchiere lamp there, and your drafting table under it."

He was so surprised by being admitted to her dream that, for a moment, he was speechless. Something was changing between them and he felt as though he was lagging behind. She squeezed his arm, then handed him the baby. "I'll go see if your mother needs help."

After dinner, when the baby began to fuss, Helen led Jeanie to her bedroom. "You can nurse the baby in here," she said. "Just relax and take your time. Drew and I need to catch up on some things."

When his mother returned, she directed Drew to sit beside her on the sofa.

"Andrew, she's lovely," she said, her eyes grave, "and that somehow makes it all the more dangerous for you. Do you know what you're doing?"

"Yes," he said firmly. He hoped she didn't ask him to *explain* what he was doing. "I have everything under control." That was a crock.

She looked into his eyes, her own softening as she caught his hand. "I know that Katherine and I have spent the past twenty years trying to protect you from gossip and teasing and the simple difficulty of having to live without your father. But you know what?"

He wasn't sure he wanted to ask. "What?"

"Your father told me that he'd assigned you to look out for *us*." Her eyes brimmed with tears as she squeezed his hand. "He says you've grown to be just the man he'd hoped you'd be when he held you in his arms the day you were born."

Drew suddenly fought tears himself. The words were like a gentle stroke right over his heart. He took a breath and swallowed. He wanted to thank her for telling him, but he knew he couldn't speak.

"I can't believe that he'll be home in two weeks," she said in a ragged whisper.

He cleared his throat. "I know, but it's finally true. Do you have everything you need?"

"I think so." She was crushing his hand. He held on, knowing part of her show of strength all these years had been bravado. "I'll buy groceries the day before he's to come home. He says he still likes all the same things—my enchilada casserole, roasted chicken, cannonball stew." Her grip on him tightened even more and she asked with sudden urgency, "But how does he know that? He hasn't had the same things, so how *would* he know. His tastes might have changed completely. He might hate everything I make."

"Mom." Drew freed his hand to move closer and put his arm around her. "He's going to love being home. And I'm sure he'll be ecstatic to eat your cooking again. Don't worry about those things."

She nodded, though she didn't seem convinced.

"I should have the car serviced," she said.

"That would be a good idea," he agreed.

"We'll all go pick him up together."

"Of course."

She laughed unexpectedly. "If Katherine has her way, Giorgio Armani himself will dress him for the occasion."

Drew laughed with her. "She means well. I think she just wants him to fit into the outside world again, and that's the only thing she can do to help."

Helen leaned into him. "I know. I've been so fortunate to have you two." She touched the shoulder of his new shirt. "And I must say, you're looking very soigné—like a designer of music centers. Congratulations, Drew. That's quite an accomplishment.''

''Thank you.'' He felt a fresh stir of excitement. Life was looking good.

''About Jeanie,'' she said after a moment, straightening to look into his eyes. ''I know you always use your head, but that becomes harder to do when your heart's involved. Remember that no matter how sad her story, it's not the truth. And that makes you wonder why she has to lie.''

He nodded. ''I'm always careful.''

''That's never been the case, Andrew,'' his mother admonished. ''You may mean to be careful, but you're usually impulsive and sometimes even reckless. Please. I'm just getting my family back together after a long, long time. Don't do anything to endanger that.''

He hugged her close and kissed her temple. ''I promise.''

''MY MOM WAS LIKE THAT,'' Julia said as Drew drove home. It was just after ten. Jeremy slept contentedly in the carrier in the back seat. ''A great cook, always knew what to say to make you comfortable and had courage to spare.''

''Mom liked you, too,'' Drew said, watching the road.

Resting her head on the back of her seat, Julia turned to study his profile. As they drove through a commercial area, light flickered across his face, highlighting the planes of his forehead, cheekbones, and chin. Drew had his mother's smile and the firm line of her jaw.

She sighed, wishing they were any ordinary couple. How nice it would be to simply wrap her arms around him, tell him she loved him, and that she and her son wanted to be part of his family.

But the situation was far too complicated to allow that.

She sat up in her seat and made the firm decision that she was going to tell him the truth tonight. He knew she was lying, but he was waiting for her to explain. She was taking a chance, but she remembered the way he'd looked at her when she'd talked about rounding out her dream with his drafting table in a corner of the conservatory. He wanted the same thing she did.

"I'll make tea when we get home," she said, dusting off her sleeve, her lap—girding for battle. "And we'll talk."

He gave her a quick glance, but didn't ask what they had to talk about. "Okay. But why tea?"

"Ah…tea is the drink of diplomacy," she said.

"Really. I never heard that. Are we going to disarm our nukes, or something?"

"I thought we'd talk treaty," she replied.

He turned off the highway onto the road that led home. "All right. I'm peaceful by nature."

She made a scornful little sound and he slapped her knee.

Once they were back in Drew's apartment, she handed him the sleeping baby. "If you'll put him in his crib," she said, "I'll put on the kettle."

"Okay." He settled Jeremy easily in the crook of his arm. "Should I change my clothes? This is my first disarmament talk. Does one wear camouflage, or is it a dressy occasion?"

She had to be candid. "You look wonderful just as you are."

After one long, lingering look, he turned to put Jeremy in his crib.

Julia went into the kitchen and filled the kettle with water. She was about to put it on the burner when Drew returned, Jeremy still in his arms.

He handed the baby back to her as he pushed her through the kitchen and into his office.

"What...?" she began to ask, but he put a finger to his lips in a shushing sound. He directed her into a closet in his office, then leaned closely to whisper, "Someone's in your wardrobe. Don't move until I come for you!" Then she was shut off in the blackness of the small space.

Her heart pounded in her chest and she held Jeremy protectively against her as panic tried to take over. Her uncle had found her! He'd sent someone to kill her and take the baby.

She pulled herself together with the thought that Drew stood between her and whoever intended to harm her and the baby.

But that was small comfort. What if the person her uncle had sent hurt Drew? What would she do without him? She couldn't imagine. It had been only seven days, but he'd so changed the texture of her life already that she hardly remembered the cold dark days before.

A loud commotion brought her back to attention and made her heart pound even faster. There was a shout, a scream, then another prolonged scream. Julia gasped in fear, clutching the baby even more tightly...until she heard shouted words in a female voice that sounded familiar.

She pushed the closet door open to hear better.

"Prove it to me!" Drew roared.

"My purse is in my car!" a woman's voice retorted.

There was a moment's silence, then Drew said, "There is no car parked downstairs."

"I just explained that! Julia's hiding and I'm undercover trying to help her build a case against her uncle! My car's parked in the back because Stanton would recognize it."

Another, longer silence, and Julia felt her whole future threaten to dissolve as Drew asked in what sounded like genuine confusion, "Who's Julia?"

"Good Lord! The woman living with you!"

Julia was both enormously relieved to recognize the exasperated female voice as Chloe's, and horrified that she'd been beaten to the punch in revealing the truth.

Bracing herself, Julia left Drew's office and followed the shouting voices to the living room. Chloe sat sullenly on the sofa, Drew standing menacingly over her. Then Chloe spotted Julia, pushed Drew aside and ran to throw her arms around her.

"Thank God! Are you all right?! Ooooh! You did have him!" She aborted her hug when she saw Jeremy, and leaned adoringly over him. "He's so beautiful, Julia. When was he born?"

Julia could feel Drew's eyes on her but carefully avoided looking at him as she showed off her son.

"Last Sunday," she replied. "Just a couple of hours after we parted company."

Chloe touched five tiny fingers visible at the end of a cottony blue sleeve. "Is he okay? Are you okay?"

"We're both fine."

"But what are you doing here? You were supposed to get a hotel room."

Julia nodded and explained.

"I was right out front here on the sidewalk when I went into labor," she said, still careful to avoid Drew's eyes. "Drew was hanging out an upstairs window, fixing a banner, and saw that I needed help. I've been here ever since." She frowned suddenly as a thought occurred to her. "How did you *know* I was here?"

"When my Caller ID showed a call from a phone booth, I called the phone company to find out where it was located, sure it was you. Thinking I'd find apartments nearby, or something, I was demoralized when all there was were shops and a day-care center. So I went into Caffeine Hy's to have a cappuccino and think about what to do. On a whim, I described you to the proprietor, and asked him if he'd seen you." She grinned. "He said he hadn't seen a very pregnant woman, but he had seen a woman fitting your description who'd recently delivered a baby. He told me you were sharing digs with Drew Kinard on the third floor of the day-care building.''

"How'd you get in?" Drew asked. "When the day care isn't open, it's a secure building.''

"The cleaning staff was working," she said with a certain pride, "and it was easy to get by them. Once I reached the apartment, I just picked the lock.''

"And it didn't bother you that that's illegal?''

"No," Chloe replied without hesitation. "I was worried about Julia. But I don't know who you are, and *that* bothers me.''

Before he could reply, Julia intercepted. She was now forced to look at Drew, but she did so with a polite smile. "Drew, this is my friend, Chloe Maddox. Chloe, my benefactor, Drew Kinard.''

Chloe glared at Drew for a moment, then smiled reluctantly. "Then you're not a complete Neanderthal. Thank you for taking care of my friend.''

He looked from her to Julia, his expression eerily cool. "Is someone going to explain this to me?''

Chloe, who didn't know that Julia had lied to him, appeared puzzled.

Julia drew a breath and said in a voice that quavered despite her attempt to appear firm, "Can I explain later, after I've spoken to Chloe?''

"No," he replied unequivocally. "I've been waiting long enough for an explanation. I'd like it now.''

"Drew, please. I—'' She began to try to reason with him, but he didn't seem interested.

He indicated Chloe with a wave of his hand and interrupted. "I take it she's not a member of the menacing Mafia family.''

"What?" Chloe asked.

Julia sent her friend an impatient glance. When it came to following a fellow conspirator's lead, Chloe was clueless. Julia went on the offensive.

"You knew all along I didn't have a Mafia husband," she accused.

He nodded. "I did. So what the hell *is* the problem?"

"She has an uncle who killed my brother, her fiancé," Chloe replied. "And who's now trying to kill her. Good enough for you?"

CHAPTER EIGHT

AFTER A MOMENT of staring at Julia and Chloe in astonishment, Drew pointed to the kitchen. "I'll put on the kettle. We're talking *now*."

Chloe shook her head as she followed Julia to the small table. "You couldn't find a sweet, complacent benefactor? You had to find John Wayne with a T-square?"

Miserable, Julia still couldn't help but smile. That did about describe him. She pulled out a chair for Chloe, then sat beside her, the baby on her shoulder.

"I was worried about *you*, Chloe. You were out of touch for so long."

Her friend nodded. "It took me forever to find this Maxie. He turns out to be a snitch Devon befriended. He lives in a deserted boatyard on the edge of Pike Place Market."

"Was he able to tell you anything?"

"He says he heard them talking and knows where they went that night she was supposed to have left for Turkey. But he won't talk. He's afraid of reprisal. Julia, I don't really have time for tea. Can you...?"

The kettle on, Drew came to join them at the table. "Who are 'they?'" he asked, "And who is 'she?'"

"They're my uncle and a woman who worked with

him,'' Julia replied. She turned back to Chloe. ''If he won't talk, what now?''

''Well, I'm still working on him. I was thinking money might be a good incentive, but I don't have any. You, on the other hand…''

''Of course.'' Julia nodded without hesitation. ''Whatever you need.''

''Wait a minute, wait a minute!'' Drew commanded, looking from one woman to the other in disbelief, then focusing on Chloe. ''You're going to a deserted boatyard at this hour to pay off a homeless snitch? You can't just…''

''Look.'' Chloe leaned toward him pugnaciously. ''I have a small window of opportunity tonight. This man has information I need to get the man who killed Devon. Now, Julia and I planned this together, and despite whatever you two have become to each other, we—she and I—have to see this to its conclusion.''

Julia saw him consider another tack. She would have felt sorry for Drew if she didn't know he was capable of the same stubbornness as Chloe.

''You don't think the police are better equipped to handle…'' he began.

''The police *are* involved. It's in Devon's notes.'' Chloe turned impatiently to Julia. ''I really have to go. Can you give me the money? There's this ratty little tug in a pile of junk put out for sale by the owner of the boatyard. Maxie wants it in the worst way. If I can give him enough to buy it, he might tell me. It's two thousand dollars.''

Julia nodded. Considering her monthly allowance, that was a small amount. When she came into her inheritance, she'd be able to buy the boatyard, the dock, and a chunk of the south side of Seattle, if she wanted to.

"Done," she said. "But are you safe going back there?"

"No," Drew put in.

Chloe nodded, ignoring him. "Sure. No problem. Maxie's harmless, and there's no one else around."

"You're certain you're not being followed?"

With an amused smirk, Chloe reached for another cookie. "I lost your uncle's goons that day and haven't seen a sign of them since. Why would anyone else follow me? You watch too much *Law and Order*."

"Chloe," Drew said reasonably, "you've been talking to snitches. I'm sure if this Maxie is willing to give you information for money, you're not the only one he does it for. I imagine word gets around."

Julia had to agree. "And the fact that my uncle's lying low doesn't mean he isn't looking for us."

Chloe shook her head insistently. "I have a sense about these things. I'll be fine. Maxie's going to tell me where Alyssa went, and I'm going to find her or her body. Either way, we'll prove the truth of everything in Devon's notes, and find out who killed him."

"Good," Julia said fiercely. "But my uncle has a lot at stake here. That's why I want you to watch your every step. Don't count on your 'sense' of things. Watch your back."

"I will. Julia, I've got to go. If the police do a sweep and take Maxie to a shelter or something, it'll take me forever to find him."

Julia handed Drew the baby. He glared at her, but took him. She retrieved the cash from her room and handed it to Chloe, who put it in her fanny pack.

"This is really stupid," Drew warned.

"Thanks for taking care of Julia." Chloe stood and patted his shoulder. "I can take care of myself." She headed for the door, Julia trailing behind.

"Are you serious about this guy?" Chloe asked as they waited for the elevator.

Though their budding relationship had just been hit with a spiked club, Julia nodded. "I am. I know it hasn't been very long. And you're probably horrified because we've just learned about Devon." She remembered clearly the love she'd felt for him, and she would always have the baby to remind her of how much they'd shared. "But with all that's happened since, it feels like another lifetime. Is that awful?"

Chloe hugged her. "How could love ever be awful? I'm sure Devon would be the last one to want you to live your life clinging to his memory. Your baby needs a father, and you need someone to love you, someone for you to love." She took a step back and narrowed her eyes warily. "But you might want to make sure about this guy. He's tough and protective, and right now that's good, but can you imagine what it would be like to live with that for the duration?"

Julia could only hope she'd have to worry about that.

"He's not as overbearing as he seems. He thought you were an intruder."

The bell pinged and the elevator door opened.

Chloe held it open. "I'll take your word on that. Don't worry, I'll talk Maxie into sharing what he knows. Does King Kong have to let me out the downstairs door?"

"No," Julia told her. "It'll lock behind you."

As the door closed on Chloe, Julia said a silent prayer for her friend, then hurried back into the apartment and went to the window in Drew's office that overlooked the play yard and parking area in back. She watched Chloe get into her small foreign import and drive away—safe so far.

Julia, however, wasn't safe. Drew was on the phone in his office, the baby in his carrier on a chair. The kettle was whistling and she would have left the room, but he caught her arm.

"Yeah," he was saying. "I know, I know. Daniel, stop telling me it's idiotic and just listen to me. My concern right now is for a pretty young woman with a Napoleon complex. She's the dead reporter's sister and Julie's friend." He glared at Julia as he said that, as though Chloe's determination was somehow her fault. "I need you to send that detective you keep on retainer to keep an eye on her. She was going out there tonight. No, I don't know any more. I'm going to talk to her now, and I'll call you back. Just send him out now. She was heading right over there. Okay. Thanks."

Drew hung up the phone, his thunderous expression fixed on her again. She hated the fact she'd hurt him, and that he'd discovered the truth in such a startling way, particularly when it had been her plan to tell him the truth tonight. But she felt as though she'd done the best she could under the circumstances, and she wasn't prepared to grovel.

At least, not until it was the only option she had left.

"Let me turn off the kettle," she said, "before it wakes Jeremy."

He released her arm and she escaped to the kitchen, taking the squealing kettle off the burner and turning off the stove.

Drawing a breath for courage, she turned to find Drew in the doorway, hands in his pockets, the carrier at his feet. There was a quiet negligence in his bearing she didn't trust. Underneath, she knew he was simmering.

She looked him in the eyes, resigned to an unpleasant scene. She was the one at fault and there was little practical defense for it.

"Go ahead," she advised calmly, folding her arms. "Say what's on your mind."

"It's too profane," he replied. "I'd rather keep it to myself until I've heard the whole story."

Funny. Her reasons for keeping her secrets sounded lame as she ran them through her mind now, but at the time, they had seemed to justify her actions.

"I'll put Jeremy in his crib."

"I'll be in the living room."

Julia settled the baby on his back in the dark room and lingered an extra moment with her hand on his warm little chest, feeling it rise and fall as he breathed. He was such a miracle. Several miracles had come to her in this apartment. She hoped heaven wouldn't recall them when she explained herself to Drew.

Leaving the door partially open, she went into the living room and sat down in the big chair at a right angle to the sofa.

Drew prowled the room, hands in his pockets, clearly too edgy or angry to sit. Silence rang between them.

"Anytime," Drew prompted.

"What do you want to know?" she asked.

He stopped and gave her a piercing glance, its message clear. *You lied about everything. Now explain everything.*

She struggled to organize her thoughts. Where on earth did she begin?

"You can start with your name," he said, going to the window and looking out.

As she stared at his back, she wondered if that was all she'd ever see of him once he heard her story. Would he simply walk away?

"I'm Julia Stanton," she said, sitting straight in the chair, hands in her lap, feet firmly planted. The mild relief she felt at being able to tell him her real name was followed by a sense of foreboding. He was going to hate her when he learned all the secrets she'd kept from him.

"Everything I told you about my parents is true," she went on, resolved to just get through it without worrying about what it might cost her. "They were Kyle and Kendra Stanton. They made a fortune in sports equipment, but both of them died when I was eleven. I was left in the care of my uncle, and he came to live with me in my parents' house.''

Drew turned from the window at that, though his features remained stony. "*Senator* Stanton?"

"Yes. I ran his campaign. I have a degree in political science from the University of Hawaii.'' She cleared her throat before going on. ''I have a monthly allowance from my trust, which he dispensed for me until I was twenty-one. My parents left him some money, too, but he went through it in the first few years. He likes women and high living when he's not in the public eye. When I was in college, he was always late with my tuition, and since I've graduated, I've been supporting the household with my allowance. He has a law practice, but hasn't been working since he got elected. My allowance paid for a lot of his campaign and supports him and his lifestyle. I think his income from being a senator finances another life in Barbados.''

Julia saw something change in Drew's eyes. He shifted his weight, but remained at the window. "I'm sorry,'' he said, without really sounding as though he was. "What was all that about him killing your fiancé and wanting to kill you?''

"I come into my full inheritance when I turn twenty-five. He wants to kill me for it,'' she said boldly. "And I think he...well, his intern's missing, and Devon was doing a story about it, and...now he's dead and there's no sign of Alyssa.''

Drew stared at her, clearly trying to fill in the blanks.

It was all so complex. With a sigh, she began again.

"Chloe and I met while taking an aerobics class at the college," she explained. "One night when her car was in the shop, her brother, Devon, picked her up. We all had dinner, then he dropped her off. We got to talking and discovered we had all kinds of things in common." She smiled wistfully as she remembered that night. "A love of Mexican food, disaster movies, tennis. I didn't get home until 2:00 a.m.

"Devon was a reporter for the *Seattle Post-Intelligencer,*" she went on intrepidly. "We fell very much in love and were engaged to be married. He disappeared in February."

"He's Jeremy's father," Drew guessed.

"Yes."

"Why all the lies?" he asked wearily.

"Chloe and I didn't know this at the time, but he'd started a story on my uncle as part of a piece on Washington State politicians. He found incriminating stuff about my uncle—evidence that he stole money from projects his senate committee oversaw. But he also found out that my uncle's intern at the capital, Alyssa Crawford, was missing." She explained about the job in Turkey that Alyssa had never shown up for.

"We don't know if she learned something and got scared and took off, or if she tried to blackmail him and he…killed her. Devon's last note said he was going to my home to look for clues because my uncle was away and Chloe and I were in New York for her birthday. Then, just about eight days ago…"

"Devon Maddox's body was found in a car pulled out of the Sound." Frowning, Drew came around the sofa to perch on the arm. She'd finally engaged his interest. "I read it in the *P.I.*"

"Yes. The story said the car had probably gone off one of the bridges. Chloe and I didn't believe it...." She told him about going to Devon's apartment and finding the disk. Then she told him what it contained.

"So you think your uncle killed Devon to stop him from learning what his intern knew? Or that he killed *her* to keep her quiet?"

"Both. As Chloe told you, Devon's notes mention that he suspects the police commissioner is somehow involved in all this."

"Good God."

"Yeah. Meanwhile, I went home to pack my things and get out of the house, but my uncle was there, planning to take me to Barbados, supposedly so I could get over Devon's death." Her throat constricted and she tried to clear it. "I think I was going to be the next one to disappear."

"But...if you've been giving him money, why would he want to get rid of you?"

"We think somebody's blackmailing him, because I was having to give him more and more money." She hitched a shoulder nervously. "I think he was trying to simplify things by getting rid of the middle man—me. If anything happens to me before I'm twenty-five, he inherits. After that, the decision's mine."

"God! He's being blackmailed by whom?"

"Devon didn't say." Her voice caught and she squared her shoulders to remain calm. "My uncle hired two men at the beginning of the year, one as a personal assistant and the other as a driver. I wanted to check their credentials, but he said he'd done it. I wouldn't be surprised if he's used them for some kind of dirty work. Maybe they killed Devon.''

His expression had softened a little, but he held himself away from her, distant.

"Anyway," she continued, "Chloe and I made this plan to search for Alyssa Crawford's body, to pick up the investigation where Devon left off. But I was within a couple of weeks of delivering Jeremy, so she took on the investigative part, and I was going to hide out in a hotel until Chloe had everything wrapped up and my uncle in jail in time for me to have the baby. But my uncle had his men follow us when I left the house." She explained about the chase in Pike Place Market. "Then I ran too far and…you know the rest.''

He studied her without expression, then said calmly, "Except why you didn't just tell me the truth in the beginning.''

"Because I was on the run," she said, surprised that wasn't clear to him. "My uncle's well-known, and well liked enough to get elected. Who'd believe me without proof? And I was afraid you'd insist on taking me to the hospital. All the records kept there would be the perfect way for him to find me. I just barely talked you out of it as it was, remember? So I made up a name and a scary husband. Everyone's afraid of the Mafia. I thought it'd make my need to hide out more credible.''

Drew leaned his elbows on his knees and rubbed

both hands down his face. She tried to gauge what he was thinking, but couldn't.

"It was a pretty pathetic story," he said.

She had nothing to say to that.

"And what you've just told me is all true?" he asked.

She was offended by the question, then realized that was silly. Why wouldn't he want reassurance? "It's all true."

"All right. Is there anything more?"

"I don't think so."

He raised an eyebrow. "You're not sure?"

"Well, I may have inadvertently forgotten something, but not deliberately."

"Okay." He pushed himself to his feet. "Forget the tea. I could use a bourbon." He headed for the kitchen.

She followed anxiously. "'Okay,' meaning everything's okay now?" she asked. "Or just 'okay'—like that's all we have to talk about?"

"How can everything be okay," he asked, calmly pouring bourbon into a barrel glass, "when you lied to me over and over?"

He put the bottle away, then countered her surprised look with one of his own.

"But...I just explained that I..."

He nodded. "I know." His voice was quiet, perfectly calm. "That you were on the run and frightened of being found out, and unsure of my reactions. I understand that."

"Then...?"

"Jeanie—I mean, Julia, I got a friend here to help

you deliver Jeremy, probably making him work against some medical disclosure code. I held you while you gave birth, I provided a safe environment for you, fed you, defended you against my sister and my mother, whom you also lied to, and helped care for your baby. I understand your lying to me in the beginning, but I don't understand why it went on."

And then he walked around her and into his office, putting his cup down on the taboret near his draughting table and straddling the stool pulled up to it—as though he intended to go to work!

He reached for a pen and she walked over and snatched it from him. He turned on the stool to watch her dispassionately. She understood his distant mood, but had it been tangible, she'd have crushed it in her hands.

"Because this is precisely what I was afraid of!" she replied, her voice and her distress rising in pitch and volume. "That you'd be angry and throw us out!"

"I'm not throwing you out," he said, turning back to his work.

She caught his shoulder and spun him around to face her. "We're still in the building," she enunciated, "but you've thrown us out of...of your life!"

"If you'd wanted into my life," he replied patiently, "you'd have given me some credit for compassion and common sense and told me the truth. And Jeremy's welcome in my life anytime."

With great difficulty she held back her tears. "I explained."

"Yes, you did. And your explanation works until

about Tuesday, then it doesn't work anymore.'' Though he didn't raise his voice, it tightened, and the flickering anger in his eyes had settled into a steady heat. "My whole life has been about the lies and mystery surrounding my father's imprisonment. I don't need more of it from the woman I'm falling in love with.''

The tears now burned in her eyes and her throat felt tight. "Then, you do want me to leave,'' she managed to say coolly.

"I want you to stop threatening to leave,'' he said firmly, "until we've put your uncle away and you and the baby are safe. Then you can do whatever the hell you want to do. Now, if you'll leave me alone, I promised to call Daniel back.''

"You know, having Chloe followed might just put her in more danger,'' she said worriedly.

He gave her that critical look she'd been getting so much of lately. "Please. I think a plan of action decided upon by a lawyer is more likely to succeed than a strategy put together by a couple of debutantes.''

"I was *never* a debutante!''

HER INDIGNATION at that suggestion amused him. And it was a good thing, because he was as combustible as dynamite at the moment, and humor, however small, helped defuse him.

"My mistake,'' he said, stabbing out a phone number. "Go to bed.''

She stormed away.

He called his friend Daniel Adler and explained

about Julia's situation and the information on Maddox's disk.

"I'll put my investigator right on it."

"Perfect. I'll meet his price, whatever it is."

There was a smile in Daniel's voice. "So the architecture business is picking up as I predicted?"

"As a matter of fact, it is. I owe you big if you can help me with this."

"We'll talk terms later. Can I call you at home?"

"Yeah. And you've got the number of my cell phone."

"Got it. You want a report tonight, or in the morning?"

"Tonight, please."

"All right. I'll ask him to call you."

"Great. Thanks, Daniel."

Drew went to Julia's room and knocked on the door. There was silence for a moment, then the door opened a crack.

Her peaked face appeared, eyes red-rimmed and swollen. "What?" she demanded in a harsh whisper. Before he could begin to feel guilty, he reminded himself that she'd lied to him long after it was necessary.

"I just wanted to tell you…" he began, and found himself having to lean closer because the door was open barely two inches.

"Could you possibly crack this thing open a bit more?" he asked.

"No," she said petulantly. "If you won't let me into your life, you're not getting into mine."

"Need I remind you that the whole apartment is mine?"

"Consider this room the District of Columbia," she retorted. "You were saying?"

"The investigator," he replied, straining for patience, "is following Chloe. I thought you'd like to know she's not out there alone."

"Chloe's not going to be happy."

"Chloe will have to live with it. Or at least I hope she gets to. This was a crazy scheme."

She closed the door on him. He tossed the bourbon down the sink and made a fresh pot of coffee, sure it was going to be a long night.

By 2:00 a.m., he was stretched out on the sofa with the last cup of coffee in the pot in one hand and his notes for the Mitchell house cum office building on a clipboard on his lap. He was accomplishing nothing, of course, because his concentration was split between Julia, looking pitiful and small in the District of Columbia bedroom, and her friend Chloe, acting like Mike Hammer somewhere in the dark night. He hoped Daniel's P.I. had been able to intercept her, or at least locate and keep track of her at this midnight meeting with the snitch.

Also distracting was the fact that Jeremy had been crying for about fifteen minutes. Some nights were like that. During the past week, Drew had always gotten up to see what he could do to help, but he doubted he'd be welcome tonight.

He was beginning to calm down a little about Julia's scheme. He'd known all along she was lying, but after finally learning the enormity of what she'd been up against, he couldn't believe she hadn't trusted him enough to ask for help. But the more he thought about the danger she faced, the less it seemed to matter how it affected him.

The telephone rang and he reached for the cordless he'd placed beside him on the coffee table.

"Drew Kinard?" a raspy voice asked.

"Yes," Drew replied.

"Toby Cornell." There was a moment's pause. "Your private investigator."

"Did you find her?" Drew sat up.

"I did. A little like putting your face in a beehive."

Drew laughed. If the guy was joking, Chloe had to be all right. Cornell didn't laugh in return. Drew tensed and swung his legs over the side of the sofa.

"Is she all right?"

"She's fine. I, however, may have a broken nose. This is going to cost you extra."

Although Drew wanted to laugh again, he didn't dare. He wasn't sure the man had a sense of humor. But, then, if his own nose had been broken, neither would he.

"I'm sorry." Drew tried to sound sober and sympathetic. "She hit you?"

"She pushed over a pile of crab pots, which hit me." Toby Cornell sighed and said philosophically, "My own fault for underestimating her. Or overestimating my own abilities. I watched her give an envelope to Maxie. They sat and talked around a fire for about ten minutes, then I followed her to her car, which she'd parked behind a pile of pots. When I got there, she dumped the pots on me."

"Can you stay with her?"

Drew expected to be rebuffed and was surprised when Cornell replied, almost with enthusiasm, "I'm parked in front of her place right now. Where is she going with whatever she got from Maxie?"

"I'm not sure," Drew replied. "Her partner in this scheme is here with me. She may come back here, or she may try to act herself on whatever she's learned."

"I'll stay with her. Anything else?"

"No," Drew replied. "Sounds like you've got it handled. I appreciate it. And I'm sorry about your nose."

"Yeah." He finally barked a laugh. "Nothing more dangerous than a woman on a mission. I follow a shapely tush and forget that every time."

"Words of wisdom." Drew felt far less concerned about Chloe suddenly. Toby Cornell was on the job. "Thanks, Toby."

"Sure, Mr. Kinard. I'll be in touch. Here's my number in case you want to reach me."

Drew wrote it on the top of his page of Mitchell notes. "I appreciate it."

He turned the phone off, reached over to the coffee table to put it down, and noticed Julia standing just inside the living room, a wailing baby in her arms.

CHAPTER NINE

JULIA LOOKED AWFUL. Her face was blotchy and swollen, her ponytail disheveled. She wore sweatpants and the T-shirt he'd lent her to sleep in that first night.

She asked him a question but he couldn't hear her over the baby's crying. When he started to get up, she came to him instead.

"Was that about Chloe?" she asked in a raised voice.

He nodded. "She's fine," he shouted back. "She saw the snitch and he's followed her back to her place. If she gets into trouble, he'll be there."

At his news, she burst into deep, noisy sobs.

God. He hated it when women cried. He was faced with it yearly on his parents' wedding anniversary. He and Katherine usually took their mother out to dinner to try to distract her, but the evening inevitably culminated with his mother weeping and Katherine crying in sympathy. He never knew what to do except hold them.

Figuring the same approach might work with Julia, Drew urged her to the sofa, then sat down beside her and wrapped his arms around her. His embrace encompassed Jeremy as well, and for the first few minutes seemed to make absolutely no difference at all.

He was about to try another approach, when Jeremy's screams suddenly became less desperate. Drew picked him up and held him against his shoulder, wondering if the baby's distress was a result of his mother's.

After a moment, the infant took several gasping little breaths then closed his eyes.

Somehow, that seemed to upset Julia further.

Drew propped his feet on the coffee table and placed the baby on his lap, tucking his little blanket around him. Jeremy didn't stir.

Calming the baby's mother wasn't going to be as easy, Drew knew. "He's all right," he said gently, slipping an arm around Julia's shoulder. "You're all right. Chloe's all right. There's nothing to be upset about."

"That's an oversimplification," she complained, still sobbing. "And you know it."

The fact that she'd used a seven-syllable word in the depths of her misery gave him hope.

"Maybe, but it's a start," he said reasonably. "We'll just have to work on the rest."

"I'm...horrible!"

"Well, yeah, but you..."

She missed his feeble attempt at humor and rolled right over him. "I'm a horrible mother! A horrible friend! And a horrible..." She paused to shake her head in emphasis. "Horrible lover!" Each "horrible" was delivered with the side of her fist to his chest.

He caught her hand and held it.

Lover? Was she coming around to his way of thinking? He knew he should concentrate on her other concerns first.

"You're a very good mother," he argued.

"No, I'm not. He's been crying for twenty minutes and I couldn't calm him down. I tried everything. But two minutes with you around and he's asleep."

"Maybe I'm boring."

She gave him a watery glare. "You've just got it together," she complained, tears streaming. "You grew up without a father at home, but you developed a sense of self and made your contributions."

He tried another tack. "Chloe obviously thinks you're a great friend or she wouldn't…"

"If I was such a good friend, I wouldn't have let her take off on her own like that—to do all the dangerous stuff by herself."

"I have a feeling," he placated, "that no one 'lets' Chloe do anything."

"She has it together, too. Devon loved her very much."

She leaned into him miserably, and he began to read something into her behavior that he hadn't been aware of before.

"Do you need to talk about Devon?" he asked quietly.

She put a hand to her eyes. "I can't imagine it would help anything."

"Maybe it'd help you."

"He's gone."

"Have you had a chance yet to understand and accept that?" Drew asked. "I mean, so much has happened—the whole thing with your uncle, and having the baby. You haven't had any time to grieve.''

She looked up at him, her expression confused. ''But I'm… I think I'm in love with you.''

All right! Drew couldn't help the thrill that raced through him, but he quickly suppressed it. There were a lot of things Julia had to work out first.

''I think it's perfectly acceptable to love me while grieving for Devon,'' he said. ''It sounds as though he was a great guy.''

Her surprise seemed to deepen. Then, swiping at her tears, she asked, ''Do you have a tissue?''

''Sorry.'' He pointed to the bathroom. ''There's a box in the john.''

''I'll be right back.'' She took off for the bathroom, then returned in a few seconds, a clump of tissues in her hand. She sat beside him and looked into his eyes. Her own were distressed and as wet and blue as the ocean.

''I think you would have liked each other. He was a dedicated reporter, determined to inform and protect the world he lived in. Just like you.'' She smiled thinly. ''You're bossy, but you extend yourself to take care of everyone around you. Your sister, your mother.''

He wrapped his arms around her again and pulled her closer. ''My father assigned me the duty when I was just a kid. It's a hard habit to break.''

''But no one assigned you Jeremy and me.''

''Trust did. You needed help and you trusted me to provide it. It's one of the world's unwritten rules.

When someone's all alone and needs you, you come through."

"And I paid you back by lying to you. I'm sorry. I'm a horrible lover." She sat up, leaned an elbow on his shoulder and looked regretfully into his face. "I know. Technically, we're not lovers. But it's another of the world's unwritten rules. When you give someone your heart, you have to be completely honest and straightforward. Otherwise, giving them your body when it's time, won't be the gift it's supposed to be."

"Gift?" He liked the promising sound of that. "Did I mention that today's my birthday?"

She giggled. "No gifts for another month or so, I'm afraid." Quickly she sobered. "It isn't, is it?"

"No, it isn't. My real birthday is September 22." He calculated quickly. "The timing should be almost right, though."

She put her hand to his cheek and kissed him with a sudden, serious ardor that pinned him in place. Instinctively one hand went to the baby on his lap in case his knees went weak, and the other he splayed across Julia's back to draw her closer to him.

It was a long and complicated kiss. At first, he had the impression the long, sensuous caress was intended as an apology. He didn't really need one, but he was happy to accept it in the form she'd chosen.

Then she dotted small kisses along the line of his jaw, his earlobes and throat. These seemed to be a sort of praise or thank-you he didn't entirely understand but was happy to accept.

Finally she stopped and leaned her forehead against

his. "I can't believe I collapsed on your doorstep. After the way my life's been going, I was sure fate had it in for me, yet...there you were."

He took her face in his hands and kissed her firmly. "Let's just count ourselves lucky."

JULIA WAS deeply, irrevocably in love. She melted against Drew once more, the three of them forming a tight little circle in the middle of the sofa in the dark room, and she decided that his take on life made sense. Don't question what they'd found together, just be grateful to have it.

"When's *your* birthday?" Drew asked with sudden interest.

She smiled as she snuggled against him. "You can't give me the present I want for another four weeks."

He laughed lightly and squeezed her shoulder. "I was asking because of your trust fund. What's your uncle's zero hour to get rid of you?"

Oh. For a few minutes she'd actually forgotten the problem of her uncle. It occurred to her that could be dangerous.

"August 29," she replied. "This coming Friday."

"Okay. Everything's going to be fine. We're going to have your uncle wrapped up so tightly for the D.A., he won't know what hit him."

Fear invaded their tight cocoon because she knew her uncle's history and Drew didn't. And now she was afraid not only for herself, but for her baby and the man she loved.

He must have felt her tension because he gave her shoulder a punitive pinch. ''I said, don't worry.''

She caught his hand and kissed it. ''I'm not worried,'' she lied.

DREW'S PLAN WAS to go on as they had been, but to leave Jeremy in the day care during the day so that if her uncle did show up, Jeremy wouldn't be easily identifiable as Julia's. Placing a baby that young in day care was against the licensing rules, but once Drew explained Julia's true situation to Katherine and Hannah, they had a quick conference and decided they could manage the small deception and put Angela in charge of him.

In order to find out what Julia was up against, Drew spent time with Devon's notes on his own computer, checking dates, activities and purchases. He told her he wanted to put together a picture of Julia's uncle, a man who'd either murdered or frightened away his intern, then killed Devon before he could publicly reveal his fiscal crimes. Drew was also in touch daily with Toby Cornell, whose fee Julia had insisted she would pay. Toby never let Chloe out of his sight. Apparently she had checked out Julia's house, where her uncle also lived, and found nothing. She was once again looking for her informant, Maxie, who'd collapsed and been treated at the hospital, then taken to a shelter.

When Julia expressed worry for her friend, Drew had reminded her, ''Toby's right behind her.''

''But you've never even met him.''

''Doesn't matter. We've talked. I trust him.'' He'd

smiled into her concerned face. "And trust, as you once explained to me, is involved in one of life's unwritten rules. When someone trusts you, you come through for them."

She'd tipped her head at him in exasperation. "Good men and women react that way, but the world is filled with people who don't."

"He's one of the good ones," Drew insisted. "I'm sure of it."

So she'd tried not to worry. With Jeremy in the day care, she spent a lot of her time there, too. Right from the start, Drew had reminded Katherine to make sure the doors were locked at all times.

"I'm not anticipating trouble," he'd said, "but Julia's birthday is Friday, and now would be the time for Stanton to make a desperate move."

His sister's face had turned white.

"What?" Drew asked warily.

"I sort of forgot. I've invited him to the opening," Katherine told him. At Drew's groan and Julia's horrified expression, she said urgently, apologetically, "Well, I'm sorry! I didn't know!" She underscored that claim with a condemning glance at Julia, reminding her that this was all her fault. "He's our senator. He lives near here, and is a proponent of child care for every working mother. It seemed like the natural thing to do."

"Has he accepted?" Drew asked.

Katherine reached for a file folder she had at hand. "He might not have." She found a sheet with a list of names and ran the tip of her pen down the list.

Then she looked up, her expression stricken. "He's accepted."

"Okay," Drew said. "No need to panic. He doesn't know Julia's here, or he'd have probably made a move already."

His sister nodded. "That makes sense."

Drew teased Katherine with a grin. "Thank you, sis. I think that's the first time you've ever said that to me." Then he grew serious again. "I'm going to plant a few of my friends at the opening, just in case there is trouble." He turned to Julia. "And you'll stay upstairs."

She'd felt demoralized and grim, but anxious to have the whole mess behind her.

The next two days she'd spent helping Carmen and the older children cut out paper decorations, bake cookies and color program covers for the opening. Her confidence came from Drew's conviction that her uncle didn't know where she was, but still, she had to battle down her fear. It would be just her ill fortune that something would happen when she finally had everything to live for. But she dismissed all fatalism in favor of Drew's take-charge optimism.

The children were down for a nap one afternoon when Julia helped Katherine and Hannah hang draperies in the five and six-year-olds' room. The two women seemed to enjoy a friendship seasoned by time and shared memories, and the knowledge that they could depend on each other. Their friendship made Julia miss and worry about Chloe even more than she did already.

Hannah was about Katherine's height, with honey-blond hair and light blue eyes. She served as the day care's accountant, but occasionally Julia saw a far-away look in her eyes, as though there was more on her mind than the company's accounts.

When the telephone rang, Katherine hurried out of the room to answer it. She reappeared in the doorway to call for Hannah.

''The bank has a question about our deposit,'' she said. ''Will you talk to them?''

''Sure.'' Hannah draped the next panels to be hung over the back of the sofa and hurried toward her. ''But my copy of the account is in your file. Can you get it for me?''

The two women disappeared. The house was nap-time quiet, and Julia simply sat at the top of the ladder and looked out at the sunny street. Trees rustled, sunlight reflecting off their leaves. Shoppers walked in and out of stores along the street, cars drove by.

When Julia saw two miniature cars racing down the sidewalk, she thought she was imagining things, She blinked and looked again.

She wasn't hallucinating. A small blue pedal car raced up the street, pursued by a similar red one. The glimpse she'd caught of the ''driver'' in the blue car looked remarkably like little Kevin Taylor, the child who'd come to visit Drew the other day.

In the red car was a little girl with short, straight black hair. Kevin, it seemed, had acquired a partner in crime.

And both were pedaling madly toward the street.

Without stopping to think, Julia climbed down the

ladder, let herself out the main door, and ran desperately in pursuit of the children.

IN HIS OFFICE, Drew looked through the data Devon had collected one more time and felt confident that fraud could be confirmed on Stanton's part. But for Julia's safety, he had to prove the murder of the intern. Stanton could be put away for the fraud, but maybe only for a short time.

He went to the kitchen for a cup of coffee, and as he passed the window, he looked out appreciatively at the sunny day. It would be fall soon, he thought, and all that would be visible from the window would be overcast skies and…

His brain stopped working abruptly at the sight of Julia running down the sidewalk, blond hair flying out behind her. How many times had he cautioned her about staying inside? What was wrong with his sister that she'd let her run out like that? And why in the hell was she running?

Because she was being chased?

Heart pounding, he tore down the stairs, too impatient to wait for the elevator. Had he been wrong in his presumption that Stanton didn't know where his niece was? Had he been overconfident because he thought he had all the bases covered? Someone watching Chloe, Daniel alerted, all Devon's info checked and double-checked?

By the time he cleared the outside door, Katherine was ahead of him, running after Julia. But there seemed to be no one chasing them. He looked up the street and then down again and saw no evidence of pursuit.

Then he noticed the toy cars at the corner, a child in each one. Even from almost a block away, he recognized Kevin. Julia had probably spotted their escape and lit out in pursuit. As he ran toward her, he saw her help the children turn the cars around and point them back in the direction of the day care.

Relief flooded through him, but he had to yell at somebody. He caught up to Katherine, who had stopped running when she saw Julia and the children heading back toward her.

"Didn't I ask you to keep her inside?" he demanded.

His sister was short of breath and had a hand to her stomach. "Julia was hanging curtains and I was helping Hannah with a phone call from the bank," she explained. "She must have seen the children through the window and taken off after them without thinking. And thank God she did!"

"OhmyGod—ohmyGod—ohmy*God!*" Amy Tidwell, an eighteen-year-old student who worked part time at the center, went tearing past them, her long blond braid and the tails of her big shirt flapping behind her. "Kevin Taylor!" Amy shrieked as she reached the cars. Kevin, unrepentant, pedaled madly toward the day care, his accomplice right behind him. "What have I told you about running off like that? And Kelly! I know this is your first day, but I was there when Carmen explained the rules to you. You must never, *never* leave the building."

The little cars pedaled past Drew and Katherine,

and Amy brought up the rear, tears in her eyes. "I'm so sorry, Katherine." She drew a breath, looking very much as though she'd rather escape in one of the little cars than face his sister. "I had put them all down for a nap, then...I wasn't feeling very well and I ran into the bathroom for just an instant. I don't even know how they got out. I had the key in my smock." She reached into the pocket of the colorful shirt she wore and looked astonished when she came up empty.

Kevin, who'd pedaled back in his car, offered up the key. "I took it when you were reading us the story before naptime. You didn't even notice."

Amy looked at Katherine in horror.

Julia joined them and bent over the blue car. "If you want to be a smart man like Drew," she said with a stern expression that wiped the smile off his face, "you have to stop disobeying everyone. You have to do what you're asked to do, and if you're bored or unhappy with the program, then you have to explain that to someone and see if there's something else you can do. You can't keep running off. And today you got Kelly in trouble, too."

Kelly, a pretty little brunette with a Prince Valiant haircut, didn't seem to mind at all.

Somewhat chastened, Kevin headed back to the day care, followed by Kelly.

"You know, you could learn something from that little speech you gave Kevin," Drew said to Julia, catching her arm and pulling her along beside him. "I remember very clearly telling you to stay—"

"Leave her alone," Katherine said, forcing herself between him and Julia and pushing him aside. "I could be looking at a lawsuit that'd bury me if she hadn't noticed the children running off—or had thought of her own safety first. Not to mention what could have happened to the children. So back off, Drew. Julia saved my hide today.'' She hooked her arm chummily through Julia's and led her back to the day care.

Drew watched them go with a terrible sense of foreboding. Julia and Katherine allied for a common purpose could not do his life any good.

He looked around him at the light street traffic and the busy shops and saw nothing out of the ordinary.

So they'd been lucky today. He could only hope their luck lasted through Julia's birthday tomorrow.

could become a target that Drew had at the
back of minds. By subtly turning off the conversation her own safety, and to distract her son,
Helen could have hoped to the chimney by back off.

Julia could see through mistake, for the second time
unobtrusively in that case, and her uncle tries to the
one side.

CHAPTER TEN

DREW PREPARED STEAKS and salad for dinner that
night, then produced a birthday cake. Julia, rocking
Jeremy in her arms, raised an eyebrow. "My birthday
isn't until tomorrow."

He nodded, looking away from her and making a
production of finding the cake server. "I know, but
there's no harm in starting the celebration early."

Julia could see through him. "You mean, in case
my uncle tries something tomorrow."

"He doesn't know where you are," Drew insisted,
producing the server. He pointed to the cake, candles
still burning. "You're supposed to blow those out."

She leaned over the cake, holding the baby to her,
and drew in a breath.

"Wait!" he cautioned. "Did you make a wish?"

The same wish was always on her mind. Safety for
all of them. Her uncle put away forever. She, Jeremy,
and Drew in the house she dreamed of on the Sound.
Or in this apartment. It didn't matter.

"I did," she assured him.

"Then, do it."

He was applauding her success in blowing out all
the candles when the apartment was suddenly invaded
by Helen and Katherine, their arms loaded with gifts.

Julia turned to Drew, prepared to scold him for forcing his mother and sister to his impromptu party, but he looked as surprised as she was.

"We heard there was a party," Katherine said, putting several gift-wrapped boxes on the table. She gave Julia a warm hug. "Happy birthday!" she exclaimed. "Can I hold the baby?"

"Thank you. Of course." Julia placed Jeremy in her arms, then accepted a fragrant, open-armed embrace from Helen. She held a large package in each hand.

"Many happy returns," she said, placing the packages on the table.

Drew watched them fuss over the baby. "Well, is anyone going to hug *me?*" he asked, pretending hurt feelings.

Katherine ignored him as she talked to the baby, but Helen went to put her arms around him. "There, there, Drew," she said, patting his cheek. "There's a new man in our lives. I'm sorry if you feel slighted."

"How did you know about the party?" he asked, getting down two more plates.

"You had Millie Gallagher bake the cake downstairs," Katherine said. "And she's just not much at keeping secrets. So, since you didn't bother to invite us, we thought we'd crash the party."

"I hope you didn't feel you had to come," Julia said, then realizing that sounded ungracious, amended quickly, "I mean, I hope you didn't think that just because…" She stopped, not sure where to go with that.

"Just because you and my brother seem to have

found something very wonderful together?'' Katherine asked with a smile.

There was no point denying it. ''Is it that obvious?''

Katherine nodded. ''And I owe you an apology. Luckily for you, I'm often wrong and have learned to admit it heroically when I am. And I was wrong to suspect you of selfish motives. I've come to like and appreciate you, and today, when you went after my children with no thought to your own safety, I realized you're a very special person. And since I seldom admit this, and will say it only once, I think Drew's pretty special, too, and I'm happy you've found each other.''

Helen put an arm around Julia's shoulders. ''I think Katherine's telling you, 'Welcome to the family.' She gets a little verbose sometimes. Now, if we could just find someone for her, there'd be happiness all around.''

Katherine raised her eyes to heaven. ''I'm happy, Mom.''

Drew handed his mother a cake plate and a fork. ''She'll find someone,'' he said. ''It might take a while, but she'll find—''

His mother silenced him with a punch to his shoulder. ''Mind your manners. You wouldn't want Julia to think we're not kind to one another. Now, come and sit with me, Julia, and tell me all about yourself.''

Julia considered this the best birthday in her recollection, despite the danger it presented. Helen and Katherine listened carefully to her story about her past, her uncle and Devon, and expressed both sympathy and concern.

Helen frowned thoughtfully when Julia mentioned her parents by name. "Kendra Stanton," she said. "I think I served on a Junior League committee with her before my husband went to prison. Beautiful blonde. Not very tall, but wore high heels all the time to make up for it. She had a lively sense of humor, as I recall."

Julia nodded fondly. "That would be her."

Helen blinked. "I don't mean to be indelicate, but your parents were worth a fortune. No wonder your uncle is so eager to get his hands on your trust fund."

"Twenty-two million." Julia quoted the figure without thought. Her parents had enjoyed their wealth but never been particularly impressed by it. And Julia had known of the approximate amount of her inheritance since her parents' death. The figure was part of her, like her height or weight.

Katherine spilled her coffee, Helen almost choked and Drew stared at her in stupefaction. "Pardon me?" he said after a moment.

"Twenty-two million," Julia repeated. Then, looking from one shocked face to the other, she said quickly, "Well, it's no big deal, except to my uncle. I just thought I'd give some to charity, travel, maybe start a business of my own."

"What kind of business?" Katherine asked.

Julia shrugged. "My degree's in political science, and I was successful at running my uncle's campaign. Maybe too successful, now that I know what he was up to. But I didn't enjoy the process or the people. My real interest lies in fine arts—I love antique fabrics and textiles, particularly old weaves, and I've picked up some courses over the past couple of years. When Jeremy's a little older, my dream is to start my own line of decorator fabrics—either reproductions or designs inspired by the past.''

Katherine seemed to like that idea. ''With all the old homes around here, people try to keep furnishings and linens true to original styles.''

''Seems as though that could be compatible with Drew's work as an architect,'' Helen said, turning to Drew with enthusiasm.

It was a moment before he reacted. He still felt in a state of shock. Then, realizing a reply was called for, he smiled and nodded. ''Could be.''

IT WAS MIDNIGHT by the time Helen and Katherine left. Julia was intoxicated by their acceptance of her, and touched by their concern for her safety. She had family!

But that euphoria was diminished by a subtle change in Drew's behavior. She knew he'd been affected by her casual announcement of the sum of her inheritance, and that confused her. From what he'd told her of his father's former partnership in NorPac, and then Eagle Aerotech, his parents had probably dealt in similar figures.

She wanted to ask him about it, but now that his mother and sister were gone, he seemed determined to deny that anything was wrong. And she had so enjoyed the evening that she didn't want anything to spoil it.

Once she'd finished feeding Jeremy, she paced the

hall outside the kitchen, gently patting the baby's back. Jeremy burped so loudly that Drew leaned out of the doorway to the kitchen, where he was cleaning up, to grin. "He's ready for football and beer," he said.

Julia cradled Jeremy in her arm, still so amazed that this beautiful baby was her son. She gazed up at Drew. Her emotional cup was running over tonight, despite the inexplicable change in him. She decided it was small enough to ignore.

"Thank you for the party," she said.

"Don't thank me." He closed the door on the dishwasher. "I know that what made you happiest about tonight was the fact that you've won Mom and Katherine over. And I had nothing to do with that. You did it yourself."

"However it happened," she admitted, "it means the world to me."

He grinned. "I hope you still feel that way when Katherine starts telling you how to dress."

"I know how to dress," she said with a teasingly superior air. "You're the only one she feels needs help."

He shook a finger at her. "Now, look. If you're going to start siding with them and ganging up on me—"

"Are you finished in here?" she interrupted.

"Yes," he said. "Why? Am I keeping you up?"

"No." She caught his arm with her free hand and drew him toward her room. "But it would be a perfect end to a perfect day if you'd sleep with us tonight."

HE STOPPED. Oh, God. How could he sleep in the same bed with her, curled in his arms, after she'd dropped that bomb about her inheritance.

He needed to think clearly. He needed to know what he was going to do.

"Oh, come on," she said with a giggle. "I just looked at myself in the mirror. It's not like I'm that seductive these days. In fact, I despair of ever having an appealing body again. It's just that I'm in a mood that has nothing to do with me physically, but everything to do with all the emotional stuff I've ever dreamed about since my parents died. I have a man who loves me, a beautiful son and a family! Me!"

Well, hell. How could he possibly deny her after that?

While Julia rocked the baby and put him in the crib, Drew showered. Then they lay together in the middle of her bed, Julia in the baggy yellow nightgown, Drew in the cotton pj bottoms he'd taken to wearing since she moved in.

When Julia curled up cozily against him, her back to his chest, her head on his shoulder, Drew thought he might go insane. But he wrapped his other arm around her and held her close.

She sighed contentedly. "This is so nice," she said sleepily.

"Mmm," he agreed. He couldn't have formed words if he'd wanted to.

She wriggled to get comfortable, her full breasts shifting beneath his arm.

He prayed for sudden unconsciousness.

"Good night," she whispered.

"Good night," he replied.

It was 4:00 a.m. when he decided he'd rather stare at the computer screen than the ceiling. After the last time Julia had gotten up with the baby, she'd fallen back into bed on her side, exhausted, and hadn't moved since. So he got up quietly, saw that she and the baby still slept comfortably and went into his office.

A thought had come to him while staring at the ceiling, and now he turned on the computer and pulled up Stanton's miscellaneous expenses column onto the screen. A list of three payments to a Dr. Fisher were grouped there. Drew had dismissed them earlier, unable to construe them as a fraudulent purchase.

But he began to wonder if they might support a crime of another sort. He dug out the huge Seattle phone book and looked up Dr. Fisher.

He found him.

Under gynecologists.

Dollars to doughnuts, Alyssa Crawford was pregnant. Considering what he'd learned about the senator, Drew felt fairly certain that lowered their chances of finding her alive. Particularly if she'd pushed him to acknowledge the baby, or made demands that might have threatened his position.

"What are you doing up?" Julia asked, appearing beside him. She covered a yawn delicately and widened her eyes as though to clear them as she looked over his shoulder. "The same old file?"

He put a fingertip to Fisher's name on the screen. "It is, but I've discovered something. Your uncle paid for three visits to an ObGyn. I'll bet the intern was pregnant.''

Julia's eyes brimmed with tears. "Do you think she's still alive?"

"I think it doesn't look good," he replied candidly.

She fell onto the edge of his desk. "How do people get to the point where they can justify killing people who get in their way?"

"Power and money are very corruptible commodities," Drew said reasonably.

"I know my uncle hated it when I turned twenty-one and got control of my allowance. That was why I offered to run his campaign, why I supported him—to remind him that I was willing to be family if he was. But all he wanted was the money. That's all he's ever wanted. And now he really needs it to pay off whoever's blackmailing him." She sat up suddenly. "I thought that was the intern. But if she *is* dead, who else could it be?"

He shrugged and took her hand comfortingly. "Maybe that's how Police Commissioner Harwood is involved. Why don't you go back to bed?"

"I was thinking I'd make some tea," she said, then kissed his cheek and gestured him to follow her. "Want some?"

He shouldn't, he thought. He should stay right here. He needed distance from her desperately. But needing and wanting were two entirely different things.

"Diplomacy issues again?" he asked, following her.

"No," she replied. "Just tea."

By the time the kettle boiled and she'd made two

cups of tea and an English muffin, the baby was up again, but apparently not hungry. His eyes were wide-open, and he stared interestedly into her face.

"He knows you," Drew observed, carrying their tea to the coffee table in the living room. They sat side by side on the sofa and she put the baby on his back on the cushion beside her. "And he's going to love being your son."

She caught Drew's arm to her and leaned her fore-head against it. "And I could grow to love being your wife. You have only to ask me."

He absorbed her words quietly. Yesterday, even this morning, he'd felt sure he could make her happy and had looked forward to the opportunity. But that was before he knew she was coming into twenty-two million dollars.

He felt the stiffness in her when he said nothing, watched her raise her head and look into his eyes, hers filled with fear. She opened her mouth to say something, but in the end simply frowned.

"You haven't heard anything new from the detective?" she asked, easing slightly away from him.

"Just what I told you. Apparently Chloe has more questions for Maxie, but she's having trouble finding him since his hospital stay." He grinned. "I hope it doesn't cost you another two thousand dollars." Then realizing that wasn't funny, considering how he felt about her money, he sipped at his mug of tea to avoid her eyes.

"You've changed your mind, haven't you?"

He knew precisely what she meant, but he pretended ignorance. It bought him a little time.

"About what?"

She closed her eyes for a moment, knowing, he guessed, that he was fabricating.

"About loving me," she said.

"No!" He denied that honestly and vehemently. When her expression grew confused, he wanted to explain, but wasn't sure he could.

"Then what *have* you changed your mind about?" she insisted, looking down at the baby. "Raising another man's child?"

That annoyed him. He didn't blame her for asking, but it annoyed him anyway. "That's a thoughtless question," he replied impatiently, certain his eyes registered his displeasure. "Do you ask it because I helped bring Jeremy into the world, or because of the number of times I've gotten up with him so you didn't have to, and walked the floor with him when he cried?"

"I ask it," she said, apparently unswayed by his annoyance, "because it's a reasonable question. A lot of men wouldn't want to raise someone else's baby."

"Well, I'm not one of them."

"Then, you just don't want to be married after all?"

A simple yes might have convinced her, but it wasn't true, so he wasn't quick enough with the reply.

She certainly deserved an answer, but "It's the money" sounded ridiculous and small. "There's an awful lot of heavy-duty stuff going on right now for us to be talking about marriage," he said instead.

"Are you afraid having a family will stall your

career," she asked gently, "when it's off to such an impressive beginning?"

"Of course not." He knew he sounded impatient, but she didn't have to know it was with himself, not her. "Now, can we just drop it until we get the police involved and your uncle's no longer a threat to you?"

She was quiet for a moment, then replied with a sigh, "Sure. Maybe by then I'll have changed my mind, too, and simplify everything for you. I'm going back to bed for a couple of hours."

She took off in a huff for her bedroom, the night-gown flapping around her ankles. Drew collapsed against the back of the sofa and concluded that the extreme cowardice with which he'd played that scene with Julia had to have been brought about by four hours of grave frustration and absolutely no sleep.

If he didn't try to get a little rest, he thought wearily, he wasn't going to be sharp enough to keep Julia safe on her birthday.

JULIA WENT DOWNSTAIRS before Drew was up again, and left Jeremy in Angela's care while she helped Kevin and Kelly and several of the other children with an art project that would be displayed at the open house. But she was saddened and distracted by the great change that had taken place in her prospects for the future. She'd thought she'd had everything she wanted last night, until Drew's cool withdrawal just before dawn.

Had she done something that made him think twice about his feelings for her? But what could it have been? She'd been sleeping! For a man who claimed not to like mystery, he certainly generated enough on his own.

She decided to push thoughts of Drew to the back of her mind until she could actually do something about him, when she found herself face-to-face with him as she got a glass of water in the kitchen.

"You could have told me you were coming downstairs," Drew said in the same tone he'd used earlier that morning. "Where's the baby?"

Julia had had about enough of him and his tone. She refilled her water glass. "I sold him into slavery," she said. "Since you're now detached from us, I didn't think you'd mind."

He snatched the glass from her. Water sloshed over both of them. His eyes told her he didn't appreciate her smart reply.

"Well, where do you think he is?" she asked, "Upstairs with Angela and the other babies."

"You could have told me."

"You were asleep."

"You could have awakened me."

"Yes, right. You were in such a bad mood wide-awake, I could imagine what you'd have been like shaken out of a sound sleep. Actually, this is the mood, isn't it? I rest my case."

Temper flared in his eyes, but she saw him swallow his anger and expel a breath for patience. "I came to find you," he said, his voice very quiet, "to tell you to stay on the grounds today. If Kevin takes off, send somebody else after him."

"I'll be fine," she assured him.

He caught her arm when she would have walked

away from him. "You will if you do as I say. And if that rankles, remember that you have a baby upstairs."

She snatched her arm from his grasp, telling herself that smacking him would not be a positive example for the children wandering in and out. "I won't forget him. I'm not the one who loves someone one day, then changes his mind the next."

"No," he replied, taking a step back from her, making an effort to keep his voice down. "You're just the one who lies all the way through a relationship."

Her voice was low but angry. "I explained why I lied!" she reminded him. "And the moment it was safe, I told you the truth."

"No, you didn't. I found out, then you tried to explain."

"Then I told you everything."

"You didn't tell me about the twenty-two million dollars."

CHAPTER ELEVEN

THE WORDS HUNG BETWEEN THEM for one protracted moment. Drew was surprised he'd said them, and Julia was obviously confused about what they meant.

"You mean that you're upset because I have money?" she asked in surprise.

That was exactly what he meant, but he knew that only indicated his insecurities, and he didn't want to talk about them now—or think about them—when she was in such danger.

His cell phone rang in the reverberating silence that followed her question. He answered it, preferring to deal with anything else rather than continue this conversation with Julia.

It was Toby Cornell. "I've lost her," he said without preamble.

"What?" Drew demanded, happy to take out his frustration on someone else. "How could you have lost her?"

"I know." There was a hesitation, then a sigh. "She slipped out the back way on me. She must have seen me."

"Toby..."

"I know, I know. But I checked the caller ID on

her phone, and the last call about twenty minutes ago was from Giorgio's.''

''The restaurant?''

''Yeah. It's across the lot from where Maxie sleeps. He must be back. I'm on my way there.''

''Okay. I'll call the police on the chance that it's Stanton or one of his men who lured her there. Call me the minute you know anything.''

''I will.'' Another hesitation. ''I'm sorry.''

''I know,'' Drew said. ''It happens.''

''What?'' Julia demanded as he punched the numbers on his phone. ''What is it? Did your investigator lose Chloe?''

He quickly explained what little he knew while he waited for 911 to pick up. ''Try not to worry,'' he said, forgetting he was angry with her. ''Toby's right behind her.''

''But he's the one who lost her in the first place!''

''She left out the back door. I think that suggests she'd seen him and was evading him.''

A deep-voiced 911 operator answered the phone. Drew told him as clearly and calmly as he could what had happened. He mentioned guns and a helpless woman, hoping it would result in enough officers to save her from harm and prevent Stanton's escape—if he was the caller.

Drew wanted desperately to go, too, but he didn't dare leave Julia. And there was the possibility that drawing Chloe to the restaurant was a carefully orchestrated move to make Julia follow. It was impossible to be sure.

The operator promised help. Drew hung up and dialed again.

Julia pulled anxiously on his arm. "We can't involve the police, remember?"

"We have to, but I know someone on the force who can help us with the commissioner."

"But..."

He put a hand up to silence her when Jaron Dorsey answered the phone. Dorsey had two children in Forrester Square Day Care and he and Drew had worked the Kiwanis Christmas tree lot together.

Again, Drew explained quickly about his 911 call and the necessity of preventing the police commissioner from getting involved.

"Not a problem," Jaron said. "He was picked up last night on a DUI with two minor girls in the car. He's not doing much police work today."

It was not the time to laugh, but Drew couldn't help it. It was nice to get a break.

"Thanks, Jaron."

"You need some help on what's going down now?"

"911's responding, but I'm sure your presence wouldn't hurt."

"Okay. Where am I going?"

Drew gave him details, then hung up.

"Isn't it this investigator's job to make sure Chloe doesn't see him?" Julia demanded as though their conversation had never been interrupted. "I mean, she knows she's in danger. What was she going to think when she noticed someone following her? That he meant her harm."

"You're absolutely right. But the police are on their way."

"You're always telling me she'll be fine. But, so far, you've done nothing to guarantee that."

"Look, I'm working with a flawed plan here," he pointed out angrily, "one that you and she concocted together, if you'll recall. You sent her out there on her own. I sent someone to keep an eye on her. I can't help that she's hiding from him."

She opened her mouth to respond, then folded her arms instead and said more quietly, "You're right. It isn't fair to blame you. I'm just upset. It isn't every day that my best friend goes missing at the same time that the man I love decides I'm too rich for him."

"God!" He swept a hand down his face. "Can we just let that go for now?"

"We can let that go forever," she snapped back at him, and stormed away.

Katherine, who stood a short distance away looking over art projects, came to him to pat his arm. "Anything I can do?"

He covered her hand. "Next time, make sure your open-house banner is secure so I don't have to hang out my kitchen window to fix it and find a pregnant woman on the doorstep."

Katherine hooked her arm in his and led him outside into a quiet corner of the yard. Across from them, toddlers played in a sandbox, a couple of preschoolers tossed a ball, while another group of kids marched around in paper hats they'd made that morning, singing the song about flowers and bees.

"Responding to people is what you're all about,"

she said gently, pushing aside the dangling branch of a mountain ash tree. "Julia's wild about you. If she's feeling tense, you have to allow her that. Someone who's supposed to love her is trying to kill her."

He leaned an elbow on the fence that surrounded them and groaned. "She seems to be dealing with that part pretty well. It's me she's having trouble with."

"Why is that? Last night it was clear she adores you."

He hated to admit it, but Katherine had always had a way of getting the truth out of him. When they'd been children, she'd used threats of physical violence, but now that they were adults, she used charm and genuine concern. Both methods were equally effective.

"It's her money," he said. "You'd convinced me she was well-to-do, but twenty-two million is pushing the envelope."

"I know. Shocked me, too. But what is it about the money that bothers you?"

He hadn't thought that through completely. He was just aware of the general discomfort the knowledge gave him. "I'm not sure. I guess that she'd be supporting us if we got married."

"Well, that's not entirely true," Katherine argued. "You're going to renovate a shrink's office and build a music center. I think most couples could live comfortably on what you'll bring in on those jobs. Her money just allows you to be able to do all the fun stuff other people dream of but can't afford."

He nodded. "That's what I mean. It'll be her money providing the fun. I want to do that."

Katherine gave his arm a punitive shake. "Andrew! What's going to count for her is that you'll be with her wherever you go and whatever you do. You'll be there to take her in your arms, to wake up beside her, to chase children with her. Who cares a damn where the money comes from?"

He wanted to believe that, but couldn't help suspecting that the day might come when she'd resent supporting him.

When he expressed that thought aloud, Katherine shook her head as though she didn't believe that for a minute. "You give one hundred percent to everyone you know and everything you do. And to people you love, you give even more than that. She'll never regret falling in love with you." She looked him in the eye with big-sister seriousness. "Unless you do something idiotic like let this relationship go because she has more money than you do."

Maybe he could try to believe it. He leaned down to kiss her cheek. "You talk as though you know what marriage is all about."

"The perfect one exists in my mind," she said. "All it needs is the right man. Heads up!"

The warning came too late. A big ball hit Drew right in the face. As the children stared at him, horrified, he sank to the ground dramatically. Katherine rescued the ball before it ended up in the sandbox, and the children swarmed over Drew, giggling.

JULIA KEPT her cell phone handy as she helped the children with their artwork, praying that someone would call to tell her that Chloe was safe, that her uncle was in handcuffs and that her life could finally go on.

She tried not to think about what she'd do. She'd have to make new plans if Drew was opting out. She didn't think she'd want to live in the lakefront house anymore. Maybe she and Jeremy would move to the east coast. She'd always liked it there. Of course, all the money in the world wouldn't make it home without Drew. And Katherine and Helen. And she'd hate not getting to meet Louis.

"Julia!" Kelly Bassett complained, snapping her out of her thoughts. "You're making my picture all black!"

Julia looked at the clown hat Kelly had asked her to outline in black. Distracted by her troubled thoughts, she'd gotten a little carried away, and now the entire hat was black.

"Kelly, I'm sorry." She hugged the little girl. "Why don't I get you another piece of paper and we can start all over."

Kevin, who was kneeling on his chair across the table, said approvingly, "I like it. Just stick some sparkly stars on it. It'll be like Harry Potter's hat."

That idea seemed to appeal to Kelly, and she reached for the stickers in the middle of the table.

Julia's cell phone rang and she left the room for the quiet hallway to answer it.

"Julia!" a voice whispered.

"Chloe?" Julia asked hopefully.

"Yes. I think I found the body." Her voice was tremulous. With excitement or fear? Julia wondered.

"Where are you? At the restaurant?"

"What restaurant?"

"At Giorgio's. The investigator and the police and everybody…"

"Julia, listen to me," Chloe interrupted. "I have to hurry. I'm at your house, and I think Alyssa's body may be in the freezer in the garage. It's covered in a tarp and there's a bunch of stuff piled on it, so I thought it wasn't working. But I followed the wire and it's connected."

"Oh, Chloe! That freezer hasn't been used for years. We just haven't gotten rid of it. Don't try to look yourself. I'll get Drew and we'll…"

There was a small scream and a sudden commotion on the other end of the line. Then Julia heard a voice she'd hoped she wouldn't have to hear again, except when it entered a guilty plea in front of a judge.

"Julia Stanton," her uncle said in a tense voice, "if you want to see this friend of yours again, you get over here *now!*"

For the space of several seconds, Julia was terrified.

"Did you hear me?" he demanded.

Then an inexplicable calm came over her. She wasn't sure how to account for it, except that this confrontation suggested she finally had the opportunity to end the limbo she'd been living in.

"If you hurt her," she replied, "whatever chance you have that I'll help you is gone. Did you hear *me?*"

"You have twenty minutes," he said.

She headed for the back door, fully intending to shout for Drew. But when she saw him in a corner of the yard with a passel of laughing children on top of him, she remembered abruptly, terrifyingly, that her uncle had already killed one man she'd loved. There was no knowing how this mess would turn out, and she was the one who'd brought it about. She couldn't bear to risk Drew, too.

Closing the door quietly, she waved at Kevin as he looked up at her from the table where he worked, then hurried upstairs to the infants' floor. She leaned into Jeremy's crib.

For just a moment she felt conflicted about what she had to do. Her son was asleep, his perfect little face no longer so pruny, the fingers of one tiny hand moving outside the blanket. She kissed his fingers, then tucked his hand back inside the covers. If she didn't finish this now, he would never be safe.

"I love you, Jeremy," she said, tears in her eyes as she stroked his fuzzy head. "Mommy's leaving for a little while, but she's going to bring you back the musical bunny she had as a baby. You're going to love it."

Tears blurred her vision as she dragged herself away, and she almost collided with Angela, who walked in with a pile of clean laundry. Julia murmured something about wanting to say hi to Jeremy, then went to Drew's truck parked in front. Last night over birthday cake, Katherine and Helen had told stories on Drew, and one of them had been his habit of keeping an extra key in the toolbox in the back of his truck. A tendency to lose his keys when he first started driving had led to the practice.

She was thankful for it now as she found the key instantly, in a little magnetic box attached to the underside of the lid. She let herself quietly into the truck, turned the key in the ignition and peeled away as quickly as possible.

KATHERINE HAD JUST LIFTED the children off Drew and sent them back to play with their ball when he heard the sound of his truck's engine. It was like the beat of his heart or the thrum of his pulse. He knew the sound on a cellular level.

"What?" Katherine asked as he ran for the building.

"That's my truck!" he shouted over his shoulder. He reached the front door in time to see the tailgate already several blocks away.

"Someone stole it?" Katherine asked in disbelief.

"Julia did."

Drew looked down to see Kevin standing beside him, a paintbrush in his hand, dripping purple paint. "I seen her," he added.

Instinctively, Drew patted the side pocket of his jeans for keys, and felt them. Then he remembered the conversation last night about the extra set in his toolbox.

Hoping against hope, Drew asked Kevin, "Did she tell you where she was going?"

He shook his head. "She was talking on the phone, then she went upstairs."

"To my apartment?"

Kevin shrugged.

Drew tried to calm down sufficiently to think straight. Had she decided his problem with her money was a deal-breaker and she'd gone upstairs for the baby and left?

He lifted Kevin's chin with his forefinger. "Did she have the baby with her?"

"No," Kevin replied.

That was a relief. For about a second. Then he realized the only other reason she'd have gone was…oh, God. Some news of Chloe that *she'd* gotten instead of him.

"You don't know who called her?" he asked Kevin.

The little boy shook his head.

Angela suddenly appeared, Jeremy wide-awake in her arms. "I heard all the commotion," she said. "What happened?"

"Did Julia just come up there?" Drew asked.

"Yes. To see the baby."

Again, hoping against hope, he asked, "Did she tell you where she was going?"

"No," she replied.

His heart sank to his feet. If Chloe had been found safe and sound, she'd have told him. The fact that Julia had raced off on her own could only mean Chloe had called needing help—which suggested she wasn't at the restaurant where Toby and the police were headed.

Panic clutched him by the throat.

He was trying desperately to calm himself when Angela said in a hesitant voice, "I overheard her say something to the baby about bringing him back the musical bunny she had as a child."

Home! She'd gone home!

Drew gave Angela a noisy kiss on the cheek. He told Katherine to call the police and tell them he thought Stanton was at his home rather than at Giorgio's. "Then call me with the senator's address," he added.

"But he lives where Julia lived."

"I know, but I don't know where that is. Somewhere on Lake Washington, near Medina, I think, but I don't know where. I'll head out that way and count on you to call my cell phone. Quickly."

Then he raced for the door, forgetting completely that he had no truck.

Daniel Adler chose that moment to pull up in front of the day care. Drew raced to help him out of his car and grabbed his keys.

"I need your car," he said without explanation. "Stay with Katherine and the kids until I get back."

"But I was…"

In the rearview mirror, Drew saw Daniel standing in the middle of the street as he raced off after Julia.

JULIA PULLED INTO the driveway of the wood-trimmed stone mansion she'd once loved so much and now felt she could never occupy again. Though that curious calm was still in place, the loneliness of the last thirteen years she'd spent here crowded in on her.

Instead of going up to the house, she turned into the driveway that led to the four-car garage, parked the car and went in through the side door. The interior was quiet and dark, the smell of oil and gasoline assailing her. For a moment she wondered if she'd misunderstood her instructions.

Then she heard shuffling behind her, and turned in time to see an overhead light go on. Chloe, her hands bound and a man's handkerchief tied over her mouth, was being led toward her between cars by Beatty, her uncle's secretary.

Absently, she noticed the dark blue Jaguar she'd left here so that it would be a while before anyone suspected she was gone for good.

There was apology and fear in Chloe's eyes, and a sort of frenzied look in Beatty's that raised the hair on Julia's neck. But her calm remained, because she'd known when she stole Drew's truck that this was no pleasantly scary adventure she'd talk about later. This was a life-and-death struggle between her and the man determined to have everything that was hers.

As Randolph Stanton came up beside Beatty, she almost felt sorry for her uncle. He had no idea that she'd acquired priceless things since she'd left here, things she wouldn't let him take from her, no matter what.

"Shorty!" he said sharply to his driver. "Hide her truck with Chloe's, then come right back."

Shorty hurried off to do as he was told.

"Julia." Randolph Stanton stepped in front of Beatty. He was tall and dark-featured as Julia's father had been. But her father hadn't lived long enough for his hair to turn gray.

"Uncle Randolph," she said calmly. "I'm here."

"I see that," he replied, then his eyes roved her from head to toe and a frown drew his brow into a V so that he turned from distinguished statesman to menacing killer.

"You had the baby," he said in a throaty voice.

"I did." Everything inside her grew cold with fear. "He's very beautiful."

He seemed to endure a dark moment, then cleared it with a toss of his head. "Well, that doesn't matter." He waved several checks at her. Long familiarity with the checks drawn on her trust fund allowed her to identify them, even from a distance. "You're going to sign these for me," he said, "then you and Chloe are going to disappear. These will wipe out your fortune on the chance anyone disputes my right to inherit and tries to claim the money for your son."

She shifted her weight and folded her arms. "How many people do you think you can make *disappear* before the world gets wise to you? Alyssa Crawford, Devon, now Chloe and me? I think you're pushing your luck."

"It isn't luck!" he roared at her with sudden vehemence.

It took all the nerve she had to hold her ground. Displaying fear, she knew, would be instantly deadly—rather than eventually deadly, which was all she had going for her at the moment.

"What is it, then?" she asked, to keep him talking.

"Boss," Beatty said, "you don't have to explain to her. Make her sign, put them in the trunk, and let's get the hell out of here."

"Shut up!" her uncle screamed again. He was clearly a man on the edge. "This would have worked if you hadn't thrown Devon Maddox's body in the lake."

"He found the Crawford woman."

"I'm not saying you shouldn't have killed him, you idiot. Just that you could have put him in the freezer, too. Or buried him. Anything else. I told you when we got rid of Alyssa that bodies thrown in water always show up someplace. But, no. Because I was in Barbados when Maddox came snooping around, you had to get rid of him your way. I had a good thing going here, and now I have to leave."

"Yeah," Beatty said dryly. "Like your life'll be so hard in Barbados."

Her uncle pulled a gun out of his breast pocket and put it to Beatty's head.

Julia swallowed, a metallic taste in her mouth.

"Be quiet, Bill," her uncle said, his voice now eerily quiet.

Beatty licked his lips and complied.

Her uncle turned to Julia. She tried not to flinch at the sight of the gun pointed at her. But Randolph didn't seem to want to talk about her.

"Your father was always the charmed one," he said. His voice remained quiet, but there was an unmistakable thread of hatred in it. "I was older, but he was the one with the easy talk, and the women and the ideas. I was the studious one, and he was into sports. Still, it didn't matter to anyone that I was working my butt off while he pranced across a basketball court. He was the one our father fawned over, the one our mother hugged when he went off to school. No one ever noticed me."

Julia listened in terrified fascination. She'd never heard him talk about her father like this before. She couldn't remember that they'd ever argued when she was a child. Her father had loved everyone. He'd left her in his brother's care, for heaven's sake.

"My father must have loved you," she said, her voice wavering just a little. "He trusted me to you. And I know he loved me very much."

Her uncle nodded, his eyes widening. "That's just it. I hated him but he never got it! He was so wrapped up in his perfect life that he never noticed. Then, to top it all off, he left me his dearest possession. You."

He spoke so gently that for a minute she wondered if he'd suddenly realized what he'd done to their family. Then he added with a coolly detached tone that made her realize he was dangerously deranged, "But he left you all the money." He sighed, as though this was such a bother. "So I had to bide my time, get what I could from your monthly allowance and wait for you to turn twenty-five."

Yes, she thought, a scary fatalism trying to sedate her against the horror of what might lie ahead. Happy birthday, Julia.

Randolph didn't just want the money because he needed it, he wanted it because it had been his brother's. The brother who'd been lavished with attention while he'd been ignored.

"Now, you're going to sign these," he said, closing the last few steps between them and taking her arm in a biting grip. He led her to a tool bench at the far side of the room and forced a pen into her hand. "Or I'll have to shoot Chloe right before your eyes."

Julia threw the pen into a pile of lumber. "I'm not going to sign. If my advantage is supposed to be that you'll put us both in the trunk of a car and dump it in the water rather than shoot us here, it's just not worth it to me. My friends will see that my son inherits, and you won't get a dime.''

"Then do it," Beatty encouraged his boss. "Show her you mean it. Do it!''

Her uncle pulled another pen out of his vest pocket. "Actually, we're through with dumping bodies in the water," he said. "We're driving this one to the car compacter at the salvage yard. If you sign these," he bargained, his voice trembling with anticipation or madness, "I'll shoot you first so you don't feel your bones crumple before you die."

She thought about her baby, safely ensconced at Forrester Square Day Care, of Drew playing with the children. If she was gone, he'd take care of Jeremy— she knew it. And he'd see that her son got her money. She felt a deep grief at the thought of them without her, but knew that was the price she'd pay to keep them safe.

"If I'm dead either way," she said, "then I'll die without signing the checks. But if you let Chloe and me go, I'll sign them."

"Okay, then." He handed her the pen.

She didn't reach for it. "Please, Uncle Randolph. I'm not the fool Alyssa apparently was. Give me the checks, let Chloe and me get into the truck and drive away. I'll leave the checks in the mailbox at the end of the drive."

"Shoot her now," Beatty encouraged. "We'll forge the damn things."

Julia studied her uncle's eyes, searching for some evidence that he remembered the orphaned child she'd been, the young woman who'd run his campaign, his niece. She saw nothing.

Shorty sidled in the door, his task apparently completed, and took his place beside Beatty.

"Sorry," her uncle said in mock apology. "Shorty's already dumped your truck." And he aimed the gun at her.

She heard Chloe's muffled gasp, turned to her friend and saw grim understanding in her eyes. Julia thought of her two weeks of happiness in the apartment above Forrester Square Day Care, and closed her eyes, prepared to go out with love in her heart.

Then the garage door blew in with a reverberating crash.

CHAPTER TWELVE

AT FIRST JULIA THOUGHT the sound was a gunshot. When something struck her in the face and she fell to the floor of the garage, she was certain. Tools and lumber flew, men ran, dust and small objects rained down on her. She lay still, waiting to die.

A commotion raged around her. Men shouted. She heard Chloe, apparently free of her gag, screaming for all she was worth.

Then she hear a man's voice calling her name. "Julia! Julia? Answer me!"

"I think he shot her!" she heard Chloe scream. "Stanton shot her!"

DREW PICKED HIS WAY around the front of Toby's Jeep, which was wedged in the hole it had made in the garage door, a sawhorse lying on top of it. While the police dealt with Stanton and his men, running in all directions, Drew trudged with Chloe through the rubble.

She pointed to a pile of lumber against a dusty window. "She was standing over there. He had the gun on her because she wouldn't sign, then she looked at me and...it was goodbye. But she was smiling."

The bullet missed, he said firmly to himself as he saw a foot sticking out from under a broken piece of wallboard. The bullet had to have missed. He couldn't have been blessed with everything, only to have it all taken away again.

He pulled the wallboard off her, and Chloe knelt beside him to help, weeping hysterically. Julia lay on her side absolutely still, her body covered in plaster dust. His heart hammered in his chest, his whole being screaming, *Please! Please!*

Although he looked for blood or any other sign of injury, all he could see was a purpling bruise on her cheek.

Easing an arm under her, he lifted her upper body and braced her with his knee. Her head lolled limply against his chest.

"Julia?" he asked.

Her eyes fluttered open and looked up into his.

"Drew," she said weakly.

"Where does it hurt?" he asked, running his free hand gently along her arms, touching her stomach, her chest.

"Where did he shoot you?" Chloe asked tearfully, leaning over him.

Julia raised a weak hand. "He was...he was aiming...at my face. Ow!" She flinched as she touched the dust-covered bruise.

Drew gently brushed the powdery stuff from around her eyes and mouth. "Well, if he was aiming at your face, he missed," he said, feeling a steady heartbeat under his hand as he touched her chest.

She blinked several times and sat up, then patted

her own body, obviously searching for the bullet
wound. She looked at him in astonishment. "I don't
think I'm hurt."

Chloe squealed and wrapped her arms around her
friend.

Drew simply knelt there and wondered how long it
would take for his heartbeat to settle down, for his
pulse to stop slamming against his temple. She was
alive. She was not only alive, she was unhurt.

He was going to kill her.

"We got everybody." Toby Cornell came to kneel
beside him. Drew had just met the private investigator
when he and Toby and the police all converged on
the house at the same time. "Stanton and both
goons." Toby studied the tearful women and asked
worriedly, "They okay?"

"For now," Drew replied.

"Good. Then we better get them out of here.
Dempsey's going to open the freezer."

Drew helped Julia to her feet and followed Toby
as he led Chloe outside. There Drew made introduc-
tions, a strange, civilized ritual considering the circumstances, but he needed something to settle his
nerves.

"Chloe, this is Toby Cornell, a private investigator
I hired to keep an eye on you. Toby, your quarry,
Chloe Maddox."

Chloe punched the P.I in the shoulder. "So you're
the one who's been scaring me to death?"

Toby raised an eyebrow, gave his shoulder one ro-
tation to test it, then studied her with hands on his
hips. He was not very tall, but built like a tank. And

when he'd driven his Jeep through the garage door, he'd proved he had nerves of steel. "You scared me a few times, too, you know. I about died this morning when I discovered you'd sneaked out the back."

"Afraid you wouldn't collect your pay?" she asked.

"No," he replied, appearing offended. "I was afraid something would happen to you. I've been watching you for a couple of days and I sort of got…attached."

Chloe looked him over from what seemed to be a new perspective. "Really?"

"Really."

She heaved a big sigh. "Well, as soon as we can get out of here, I could use a cup of coffee."

"I'd be happy to see you get one," Toby said.

Through the hole in the garage, they could hear snatches of conversation and the sound of articles being moved off the freezer. "Watch your head." "Give me a hand. This is heavy!" "That's it. Now get the tarp off."

Suddenly everything fell silent, and Drew could only guess they were opening the freezer. Julia took a step backward when they heard the collective gasp.

He caught her arm to steady her.

"I wanted us to be wrong," she said, her voice thick. "I wanted her to be safe somewhere."

Drew knew how she felt. The harsh confirmation of everything they'd suspected was going to be harder to deal with than they'd imagined. Chloe was pale and had raised a fist to her mouth. Toby put an arm around her.

Jaron Dorsey wandered out a few minutes later. "It is Alyssa Crawford." The detective looked from one woman to the other. "Who's Chloe Maddox?"

Chloe raised her hand.

"Good work," he said. "Thank you."

"We're betting the autopsy will show she's pregnant," Drew said, "and that the baby is the senator's."

Jaron nodded. "Everybody all right?"

The four of them assured him they were fine.

"I'll need your reports, but that can wait until tomorrow. Why don't you go home now? I've called for the medical examiner and this is all going to take a while. Oh, and Drew?"

"Yeah?"

"The commissioner *was* blackmailing the senator. You were right. He admitted it when the D.A. promised him a deal if he'd testify against Stanton."

IT WAS OVER, Julia thought. The knowledge that her own flesh and blood had been part of such a vicious circle of events blunted her satisfaction. And the hard lines of Drew's face weren't doing much for her hope for the future.

He'd come after her, true. But that had probably been simple compassion. He'd shouted at her once for not giving him credit for that. But he didn't look at all as though he wanted to keep her now that he'd found her.

"Well," Toby said to Chloe. "You want to get that cup of coffee?"

She smiled at him. "I do." Then she turned to Julia

and they shared a look that seemed to encompass happiness, grief and all the other emotions they'd shared since Devon Maddox's body had been discovered. They held each other for a long moment, then Chloe freed Julia and came to wrap her arms around Drew.

"Thank you for coming to find us," she said solemnly. "I was sure we were goners."

"You've got to learn to trust," he said, hugging her in return.

"I was involved, too, you know," Toby said as he led Chloe away. "I could use a hug."

As their voices faded away, Chloe could be heard to say, "And you'll get one if the coffee's good."

Julia had never fainted in her life, but right at this moment, she felt she was close. Considering all she'd been through in the last two weeks, she had every inclination to simply go with the impulse to unlock her knees and let whatever happened happen.

But Drew's thunderous face suggested she stay on her toes. She wanted to hug him as Chloe had done, to tell him what it meant to her that he'd come in search of her when she'd run off without a clue. But he didn't look as though he'd welcome touch on her part. She also didn't think that trying to explain that she'd had his best interests at heart when she took off would placate him.

She didn't know what to do, but she didn't think she could remain standing here any longer. "Can we go home?" she asked.

Then it occurred to her that the threat had been lifted. He might consider that the apartment on the third floor of 10 Sandringham was no longer home to her.

Her heart thundering in her chest, she waited for an answer.

"Have you got the rabbit?" he asked.

She *was* losing it. "What rabbit?"

"The one you promised Jeremy you'd bring home to him," he explained. "The musical one you had as a child."

When she looked surprised that he knew, he said, "Angela overheard you telling Jeremy. That's how I knew where you'd gone."

The pulse in her throat was choking her. "You came after me."

He nodded once without smiling. "Did you really want the rabbit? I'm sure Jeremy will never know you broke a promise if you don't want to go in."

"I went to tell you my uncle had threatened Chloe," she said, "but you were in the backyard with little kids all over you, and I thought, 'Even if he doesn't want to raise Jeremy and have children with me, he should survive to have them with someone else.'"

His features hardened and he caught her arm and led her toward the house. "You were angry with me because I was...confused...about the money." His voice was tight and low. "So you took off without telling me, knowing I'd freak when I found out, just to show me you could hurt me, too."

She stopped, horrified that he could have so misunderstood her intentions. "How could you think that?"

He pulled her along with him toward the house. "Because that's what you intended. At least I didn't hurt you deliberately."

Anger replaced her general terror over the events of the day. It felt curiously good. "Letting some testosterone-driven idea that a man should make more money than a woman stop you from loving me and Jeremy is as deliberate as it gets. Not to mention lowdown, low-browed and just plain low."

She marched on ahead of him, but he caught up with her at the foot of the wide steps that led up to the front door. He turned her around to face him. "It wasn't deliberate. My family had money, we lost it, we struggled, we endured. I like what we've become."

"I thought you loved me," she said, looking up in to his face.

"I *did!* Until you—"

"Just stop the accusations for one minute," she interrupted, "and think about what you just said. I had money the whole time you loved me, you just didn't know I did. Your indignation isn't because I'm loaded, it's because you think it threatens your manhood."

He bristled, looking predictably male. "Nothing," he said, "threatens my manhood."

"This behavior does," she retorted, and ran up the stairs.

The front door gave under her tug and she walked into the slate-tiled corridor and stopped. Her intention was to run up to her room, snatch the bunny from the brocade settee where several old toys still sat and run back down with it while trying not to notice the house. She didn't want to be here—could never live here again.

But instead of her uncle's coldness, she was suddenly warmed by memories of coming home from school before her parents died—being greeted by her mother, often with a party of her friends visiting over coffee.

She took several steps inside and turned her head toward the sitting room where they'd all retreated after dinner, her father in a big chair by the fireplace, reading the business news. When she'd been very small, if she'd brought him a book, he'd put the paper aside and lift her into his lap.

It was almost unbearable knowing that his brother had envied and disliked him all of his life.

A happier image was her mother on the stairs in a ball gown, leaving for some charity event, her father in a tux in the downstairs hallway, encouraging her to hurry.

At the sound of footsteps behind her, she turned, half expecting to see one of them.

It was Drew, and he was clearly awed by his surroundings—the antique furniture, hand-woven rugs, valuable artwork adorning the silk-lined walls. The ceilings were high, their architectural details ornate.

"Quite a place," he said, looking up at the paintings of birds and flowers above their heads, apparently forgetting he was furious with her. "I have a vague memory of our home before my father went to jail. It was roomy and beautiful, but this is something else. That ceiling isn't Gallant, is it?"

"It is," she replied. "This place belonged to a lumber baron in the old days."

He followed her as she walked toward the staircase. "Look at that," he breathed in wonder, putting a reverent hand to the inlaid wood on the balusters. "You just don't see that anymore."

"You admire," she said, "and I'll go get the bunny."

She hurried upstairs to her bedroom, trying not to notice the room where she'd had such a happy early childhood, then such a lonely adolescence. She picked up the frayed bunny, his terry-cloth body still soft after years of handling, and turned the key hidden in his back.

A somewhat tinny rendition of Brahms' lullaby filled the room, and the years she'd had with her parents came back to her with all the warmth and love she'd known. She clutched the bunny to her, trying to capture the feeling to take back to Jeremy.

A deep sob rose out of her. Not pain, she realized in surprise, but simply emotion needing an outlet.

Strong arms wrapped around her from behind and held her close. "It's all right," Drew whispered, kissing her cheek. "I'm sorry it was so awful, your life with him, this day. But it's over now. He's gone."

And in that moment, her past and present converged, squeezing out all the sadness she'd endured.

She turned in Drew's arms and held on to him, absorbing the warmth and comfort of his strong embrace while the bunny played on.

"Come on," he said finally, taking her hand and leading her toward the stairs. "Katherine and everyone else at the day care will be going crazy. And I stole Daniel's car right out from under him to follow you.''

''Daniel?''

''My lawyer.''

''You didn't notice what happened to my Jaguar, did you?'' They walked across the lawn and back to Daniel's car, parked several yards from the garage.

''Ah...animal or automobile?''

''Automobile.'' The ME's vehicle had arrived, but the police cars with her uncle and his cronies were gone. ''And why did Toby drive his car through the garage door instead of walking in?''

''He and I got here at about the same time, but he had pulled right up to the garage. We looked in the side window, saw the situation was desperate, and decided we needed a diversion. Toby volunteered his Jeep.'' Drew grinned. ''I was driving Daniel's car, after all.''

They weren't allowed very close, but Julia could see her Jaguar crunched between the Jeep and the side wall of the garage. The rear bumper had been neatly accordion pleated.

She sighed. She'd bought it for herself when her uncle was elected, thinking that even if he didn't appreciate her skills, she could congratulate herself.

''I'm sorry,'' Drew said, pushing her gently toward Daniel's car. ''But you couldn't very well take Jeremy around in that. He's supposed to be in the back seat, and it doesn't even have one. And you'll never get a T-ball team in there.''

''I suppose you'd be happy to help me shop for

some big SUV?'' She wasn't sure what they were doing. He was kind and comforting, but she could tell that his anger hadn't entirely dissipated. He was talking about her future, but hadn't put himself in it.

"Maybe something not quite so big," he said, letting her into the car. "Incidentally, where's my truck?"

"I'm not sure. My uncle had his driver move it to wherever they'd taken Chloe's car so it wouldn't be seen. Probably into the woods on the other side of the house. There's a trail wide enough for a car for a few hundred feet before the trees close in."

He came around to slip in behind the wheel. She patted his knee. "I'm sorry about the truck. If it's damaged, I'll buy you another one when you help me pick out a new car. That is, if it won't somehow inhibit your masculinity to let me do that."

The key was in the ignition, but he gave her a berating glance before turning it. "Careful, okay? My mother and sister have managed to civilize me, but today that's just a thin veneer over the kid who learned to defend himself against all the teasing about his jailbird father."

"I'm sorry," she said sincerely. "And you did just put that guy behavior to good use when you broke into the garage, so I shouldn't grumble about it."

"Thank you." He handed her his cell phone. "Call Katherine and tell her you're okay, and that your uncle's on his way to jail."

THERE WAS MUCH REJOICING when they reached Forrester Square Day Care. Katherine, Helen, Hannah,

Carmen and a man Drew introduced as Daniel Adler, the owner of the car, came out into the street to help them out of the car and hug them gratefully.

Inside the day care, Kevin wanted all the details of the rescue, and the other children clustered around to hear. Julia admired the way Drew made the story exciting without any reference to the violence or the horrible reason that had led Chloe there. He emphasized how valuable the information was that Kevin and Angela had given him.

While Drew answered Kevin's questions, Julia took the bunny to Jeremy. Angela hugged her with relief. ''Thank God you're safe!'' she exclaimed.

Julia hugged her back. ''Thank God you heard me tell Jeremy I was going to return with my bunny. I thought I wanted to take the risk alone, but I was very grateful when Drew showed up just in time.''

Angela nodded sagely. ''I know. We can do everything men can, but sometimes the situation requires muscle as well as brains, and it's nice to have a big guy on your side.''

That was certainly the truth. Julia took Jeremy upstairs to Drew's apartment, needing to hold him, and feed him. She sat in a corner of the sofa and turned the key in the bunny. While the music played, she told her baby about his grandparents—and how determined she was that Drew was going to be his father.

DREW CAME UPSTAIRS to find Julia and Jeremy asleep on the sofa, the musical bunny still playing his tune.

He sat beside them, wrapped his arms around both of
them and said a prayer of gratitude for the first time
since he'd refused to go to Sunday School in the fifth
grade.

CHAPTER THIRTEEN

DREW AWOKE with the conviction that he and Julia had to straighten things out between them today. They'd slept together in her bed, Julia snuggled in his arms, but she'd been too exhausted to talk. Everything still lay unresolved between them—his attitude about her money, her tendency to keep things from him.

The sound of female voices drifted in from the kitchen. His mother and his sister—and another voice he couldn't quite place, except that it was familiarly strident. He looked at the empty crib and decided he had to marry Julia, and quickly. No way was poor Jeremy going to endure the same exclusively female influences he'd put up with.

After a quick shower, he put on jeans and an old blue sweatshirt, remembering that he had to string lights in the yard for the open house this afternoon.

When he walked into the kitchen, he found Julia, his sister and his mother, the baby on her shoulder, sitting around the table. Occupying the fourth chair was a young woman with mousy features, dressed in a silky chartreuse blouse. Four or five gaudy bracelets adorned her left wrist, and in her right hand she wielded a pen over the many clippings, photographs and notes spread out on the table.

Drew recognized her as Debbie North, a reporter for the *P.I.* Once she found out that Louis Kinard was going to be released this year, she'd become fascinated by the case. Drew figured she was planning to do a big feature on his father for her paper. Over the past months she'd shown up in the damnedest places, always full of questions. The front seat of her car was a mobile office, including a file box filled with research on his father's case.

She annoyed him something fierce, but his mother and sister seemed willing to tolerate her, insisting that she was sympathetic to their situation. And it was Katherine's contention that by digging into the past, the reporter might one day prove their father innocent.

Drew agreed with that to a point, but he hated the thought of their father being faced with her nagging questions and the inevitable publicity when he was probably anxious to put the past behind him and reestablish a normal life.

"This is from the July 20, 1983 *P.I.*," she was saying. She held up a clipping from the paper in one hand, and in the other, the photograph of an antique crystal cross stolen from Our Lady of Mercy Church during a robbery that had taken place the same night as the fire. "I have a hunch the two things are related. If we can figure out how, I think it'll lead us in the right direction."

"Do you think they're related?" Katherine asked.

"It'd be strange, to have two such dramatic events that weren't related happen on the same night in such an upscale and usually quiet neighborhood," Debbie suggested. "Not impossible, maybe, but strange."

She noticed Drew standing in the doorway. "Good morning, Mr. Kinard." She always called him "Mr." because she knew he resented her constant questions.

"Good morning, Miss North." He went to the coffeepot and saw that someone had left him an empty mug and a maple bar. "No scandals here today, just an open house. You aren't going to spoil my sister's big day, are you?" He took a bite of the pastry while pouring his coffee.

"I'm just trying to get to the bottom of the mystery," she said. "And I stopped by because I know your father's going to be released very soon, and I thought it would be wonderful if we could greet him with proof that he's innocent. Julia was kind enough to allow Katherine and Helen and me to come up here and talk things over privately."

"He's served twenty years for the crime," Drew pointed out, leaning in a corner of the counter. "I'm not sure if proving his innocence would comfort him or send him over the edge."

The reporter began to gather up her notes and clippings. "I think he'd be happy to be exonerated."

"I think he'd be happy to be left alone."

His mother frowned at him. "We do appreciate your interest in my husband's story," she said. "But I think Drew's right in believing he'll want some privacy at first. You can call *me* anytime, though, and I'll meet with you when I can."

"Just don't bother her at home," Drew added.

His mother's frown grew darker. He met it intrepidly.

"Thank you, ladies, for your courtesy," Debbie

North said, hoisting up her bulging briefcase. She stood to reveal chartreuse pants that matched the shirt, and sequined chartreuse slip-on shoes. Drew couldn't help but wonder how a woman so determined to find the truth couldn't see it when she looked in the mirror. And his sister thought *he* dressed badly. ''Goodbye, Mr. Kinard.''

''Goodbye, Miss North,'' he replied politely.

Julia walked her to the door.

''That was rude,'' Katherine accused as he came to take the now empty chair. ''She's trying to find out what really happened.''

''She's trying to make a name for herself as a reporter,'' he corrected. ''She's not as interested in Dad as she is in her own reputation.''

''How do you know that?''

''Because if she had any real concern for us, she wouldn't show up to bother Mom after church, or me at the gym, or you on the day you're having your open house. And don't try to tell me she didn't know it was today. She knows everything about each one of us.''

''That's just plain paranoid.''

Julia returned to the table and resumed her chair. She looked at Drew. ''Debbie said to congratulate you on being asked to design the Wyatts' music center.''

Katherine stopped, her coffee cup halfway to her lips, as Drew sent her an I-told-you-so look across the table.

The conversation shifted to a less controversial subject—the open house—and Katherine took Julia and Jeremy with her when she went to work, explaining that she needed help with the children's hats for a musical number they would perform.

Drew realized his opportunity to talk to Julia would have to wait. "I'll be down soon to string the lights."

"Great," his sister said.

"What's the problem?" Helen asked the moment the door closed behind her daughter.

"With Katherine?" Drew was determined to sidetrack her. He didn't want to discuss what he didn't have an answer for. "Well, you know we've been wondering that for most of my—"

She rapped his knuckles with her spoon. "I mean with you and Julia. Doesn't having her back safe and sound erase whatever issues you had with the fact that she lied to you, and that she has money?"

He closed his eyes. "Oh, God."

She hit him with the spoon again. "Don't 'Oh, God,' me. I want this family together and solid by the time your father comes home. And that includes Julia and Jeremy."

Drew took the spoon from her and tossed it at the sink. It landed with a clang. "Mom, I love you. But you cannot determine what are issues for me and what are not. I…"

"You're upset because she took off in your truck without telling you. I know. She explained it to me. But she did it with the best of intentions, and if you would put that male pride aside, you'd see that."

"It isn't male pride!" he insisted, raising his voice. She gave him the same look she used to give him when he was in his teens. He lowered his tone a notch. "She did it to terrify me and it worked."

"She did no such thing," his mother insisted. "And don't tell me it isn't a matter of male pride. You have an overabundance of it. You've fought my influences all your life, and Katherine's as well, and you've overcompensated by becoming this very sweet, but very authoritative man. Give me a break, Drew, and get off your high horse. Your father's coming home and he's spent the past twenty years with other men with attitude. If I have to deal with two of you, I'm leaving for Betty Ford."

He raised an eyebrow. "The Betty Ford Clinic is for people fighting addictions."

"That's what I'll be doing by then." She downed the last of her coffee, pushed away from the table, and went to the doughnut box on the counter. "Do I have to fight you for this last maple bar?" she asked.

"No," he said. "It's mine."

She ripped it in half, handed him one of the pieces, then let herself out of his apartment.

He heaved a sigh and thought he deserved another cup of coffee before he tackled the lights.

THE OPEN HOUSE WAS a rousing success. Client parents and prospective clients came and went all afternoon and evening. Excited children dragged their parents from room to room, showing off their cubbies, artwork and games, and the piano they all loved to gather around to sing.

Friends dropped in with good wishes, and Chloe came with a schefflera in one arm and the other hooked through Toby Cornell's. It gave Drew great satisfaction to see her safe, and Toby looking as though something wonderful had happened to him. Drew had known him for only a short time, but they'd stormed the barricades together, so to speak, and he liked the P.I. Drew pointed them toward Julia, who was serving refreshments in the kitchen.

Jordan Edwards stopped by with an armload of pom pom chrysanthemums in a cloisonne pot. He handed Drew the flowers. "This is heavy," he said, his arthritic hands helping to steady the pot as Drew took it. Except for his disfigured fingers, the tall, slender, white-haired man looked as hale and hearty at seventy as he had the years Drew was growing up. And tonight, in a suit, he had all the debonair charm of a seasoned Lothario.

Jordan hugged Katherine, then Helen. Drew went to find a safe place for the pot, finally settling on a high shelf in the office.

In the hallway he was accosted by Carlos Vega, Katherine's foster son, who grabbed his arm and dragged him to a kitchen window. The room was momentarily empty.

The flip in the front of Carlos's buzz-cut brown hair stood up smartly for the occasion, and his dark eyes were bright as he pointed out the window.

"What about Daniel for Katherine?" he asked, indicating the lawyer in conversation with Drew's sister in the backyard. "They get along good. She trusts him."

Carlos turned to Drew for his opinion. The gangly twelve-year-old had recently began a quest for a husband for Katherine, wanting to make her as happy as she'd made him, Drew suspected. Carlos often consulted him on the subject.

Drew shook his head regretfully and clapped Carlos on the shoulder. "Nice try, but I don't think so. Daniel's great, but he works all the time. And we want someone who'll put Katherine first, give her his time."

Carlos sighed disconsolately. "I can't leave and marry Christina Aguilera," he said, "until I know Katherine's got a man who makes her happy."

"Keep trying," Drew advised gravely. "I'm sure we'll find her someone before you're out of college. You can't leave before then, anyway."

Carlos punched his shoulder lightly in return. "Thanks, dude. I'll keep on it."

"Good man."

When Drew went back outside, Carmen had gathered the children into a semicircle, three children deep, and they were singing that song about bees and flowers that even he was beginning to learn the words to. The rendition was enthusiastic but off-key.

"We could really use a music teacher," Julia said, coming up beside him.

"We?" he asked.

She nodded. "Katherine's asked me to get accredited so I can help out for a while. It'll keep me busy until I can get my fabrics idea off the ground, and it'll be a great place for Jeremy."

He often had difficulty figuring her out, so he shouldn't be surprised by anything she said. "I would think it'd take a lot of your time to manage twenty-two million dollars.''

"Oh, that," she said. "I gave it away."

He didn't even bite on that remark, sure it was intended to bring up the subject of their disagreement. Now wasn't the time.

She folded her arms and watched the children. "I decided that you, difficult as you are, are more important to me than the money, so if you hate it, then I don't need it."

Seems he had to play the game. "Who'd you give it to?"

"Maxie. Daniel's going to see that he gets it."

Okay, this was getting a little too out there, even for her.

"Relax," she said. "I only gave him a hundred thousand. Set him up in an apartment. Put Toby on the trail of his daughter. The rest is in trust for Jeremy."

JULIA WAS suddenly being led at a run across the backyard, through the day-care building and out the front of it, where knots of visitors were sipping punch and talking. Drew didn't stop until they were halfway up the street and the crowd had thinned out.

It was dusk, the night was warm but with a subtle suggestion of fall. The air no longer smelled of flowers, but of grass and ocean.

He backed her up against a big-trunked mountain ash, a comb-shaped leaf here and there already turning gold.

"I don't know if you're joking or serious," he said.

His eyes, which had been kind, but had kept her at a distance all day, were now darkly intimate.

She inclined her body toward his, unable to stand another moment of this careful dance. "Which one will make you kiss me?"

"Julia."

She reminded herself that she'd once hoped she'd have to deal with a lifetime of this man's stubbornness. So it was time to learn.

"Daniel's helping me put twenty million in trust for Jeremy," she said. "We talked about it while you were stringing lights. He's a wonderful man. You could learn some fashion tips from the way he—"

He put a hand over her mouth. "Stop being glib," he directed, "and just talk to me."

She kissed his hand, then pulled it down. "That leaves us with a little under two million, and you're just going to have to live with that. Jeremy and I will be busy here while you put up brilliant buildings all over Seattle. But when it's time to take a vacation or buy something we really, really need, we'll dip into the savings, and you're not going to make me feel guilty that we have it. Okay?"

He looked concerned.

"What?" she demanded. "I thought that was fair."

Taking her face in his hands, he said softly, "It's more than fair. I just had to come to terms with not being everything you need…financially, I mean."

Her impulse was to react explosively, but she remembered in time that she was learning to get along with him. "You saved my life against very difficult odds,'' she reminded him quietly. "No fortune either of us had could ever mean as much as that."

He kissed her, devoured her, reached into the bottom of her soul, and for that moment, at least, they were one.

"I love you," he said, his voice thick as his lips moved from her mouth to her throat. "I love you."

She tightened her arms around him and kissed him with the same fervor. Then she pushed against his shoulders to wedge a small space between them so she could look into his eyes. She'd been thinking about this all afternoon.

He waited warily.

"I love the apartment," she said, running her fingers through his wiry hair, "but Katherine signed up eleven new families tonight and she's probably going to need the room."

"Yeah?"

"How would you feel," she asked hesitantly, "about...moving into my house?"

He blinked. "You mean...the mansion?"

"Yes. See, I didn't think I'd ever be able to go back there. All I could remember were the years with my uncle, and how cold and lonely it was. Then... then we went in together, and I remembered how it used to be when my parents were alive, and what a wonderful place it was. And I think that was because you were with me. That maybe..." She kissed him quickly, hoping his reaction would be fueled by the interest he'd shown in the place's architecture, rather than his aversion to her money. "Oh, Drew. Couldn't we raise Jeremy there? And a few other children?

Couldn't you fix the porch in the back to be a conservatory, like at your mom's, and wouldn't you love having an office in one of the upstairs bedrooms? They're huge. You'd have lots of room. And at Christmas, your parents and Katherine and Carlos could come and stay with us.''

She was chattering, but he was smiling, and when he cut her off with a kiss, she felt approval in it. ''Yes,'' he said. ''I'd love that.''

EVERYONE HAD GONE. The building was quiet again and had that expectant atmosphere Drew was always aware of when the children weren't there.

But in his apartment, there was no waiting. He'd spent the last hour in the middle of the sofa with the baby in one arm and Julia in the other, making plans for a fall wedding.

''You think anything will come of Chloe and Toby?'' Julia asked lazily.

''I like him,'' he said, then kissed the top of her head. ''Chloe, however, has all your bad habits.''

Julia slapped his stomach where her hand rested. ''I thought we decided to forgive each other for our bad habits.''

''We did, but we still have to learn to live with them. I have the advantage of having grown up with women. If Toby has a single father or a bunch of brothers, he's dead in the water.''

''If you keep this up, we may not celebrate your birthday at all when the time comes. No party, no cake and no *gift*.''

As he kissed her soundly in apology, the phone rang. He reached for the cordless on the coffee table.

"Drew, it's Jaron." Although his friend's voice was steady, Drew thought he detected an anxious note in it. "Stanton got away from us. He was being taken from the jail to the courthouse for a quick arraignment. It was late—he knocked out the deputy accompanying him and took off."

Drew swore and handed the baby to a worried-looking Julia.

"I'm sending a car to watch your building," Jaron said, "but I'm sure we'll find him before he gets that far."

The words had barely been spoken when there was the sound of glass breaking downstairs. "Tell the car to hurry," Drew said, getting to his feet. "I think someone's just broken into the day care. I'll lay you odds he's here."

He pulled Julia to her feet and led her as far from the window as he could. "Stanton got away," he said, going to the window himself to look for some sign to indicate just where Stanton was. Then he saw a curious, dancing light on the sidewalk. He swore again.

"How did he get away?" Julia demanded as he pulled her with him to the door. "Where are we going?"

"He just set the first floor on fire," he said, redirecting her when she would have gone to the elevator. "Down the stairs."

They had reached the first floor when the stairway door burst open, and Randolph Stanton appeared with the kind of shotgun kept in police cars. Once he'd knocked out the deputy guarding him, he must have escaped in a police unit.

Drew pointed Julia down the stairs. "Go," he said. "Go down into the underground."

As he spoke, Randolph took a bead on Julia. Drew rushed him, praying that for once, she'd do as she was told.

The older man smelled of perspiration and kerosene as they fell together into the open doorway. Drew heard the crackle of flames, felt their heat.

"You ruined everything!" Randolph shrieked at Drew as they struggled. "*She* ruined everything! And you're going to pay!"

Drew took a hard blow to the jaw with the butt of the gun before he managed to wrestle it from Stanton and toss it away. It must have fallen into the flames because he heard the ammunition explode.

The man was strong and fit for his age, but it was easy for Drew to remember all he had put Julia through, to recall his innocent victims, Alyssa Crawford and Devon Maddox. With renewed determination, Drew fought for all he was worth.

He didn't know if it was the sound of sirens or the blow to the head he'd just taken, but he heard ringing.

COUGHING FROM THE SMOKE, Julia pushed her way into the basement of the day care, then through the makeshift door that separated it from Seattle's famous underground. The tunnel smelled moldy and dank, and was filling with smoke. She shielded Jeremy against her as she made her way through it, worried about how much his little lungs could take.

Then she saw a flashlight dancing off in the distance and headed toward it. With a start, she stumbled against someone. She could smell him before she could see him through the haze.

"Sorry, miss," the man said. He was tall, with long gray hair and a full beard and mustache. A green nylon bag was gripped in his arms, and he looked frightened, disoriented.

A homeless person, she guessed. She'd heard that a lot of them lived in the tunnels, but had never seen it for herself. Now several others shoved past him, clutching possessions, one leading a mongrel dog on a rope leash, another running with a child by the hand, all heading toward the beam of the flashlight.

"Follow me," Julia told the bearded man. "It's all right. I think we're almost out of here."

He looked around him, clutching his bag.

"This way!" a voice shouted. "Follow my light. Come on. This way!"

Julia pinched the sleeve of the bearded man's coat in her fingers to make sure he followed. She made her way toward the light, half her attention focused on protecting Jeremy from the smoke, and the other half terrified about what was happening to Drew. He was younger than her uncle, but Randolph Stanton had hatred and vengeance on his side.

She told herself firmly that Drew would be all right. That they wouldn't have survived yesterday, only to lose each other today.

A police officer materialized out of the smoke and came to take her arm. "You're almost to the street, ma'am. Just keep coming. Is the baby okay?"

In response, Jeremy began to scream.

The officer smiled. "I guess so. But have a paramedic look at him, just in case. Come on, buddy," he said to the homeless man. "Just keep walking."

They reached a set of stairs and came up into the blissfully fresh air. Julia was surprised by the sight of so many firemen and police officers and the scores of street people streaming out of the smoky tunnel. Fire trucks and police cars filled the middle of the street.

Julia spotted tall, blond Jaron Dorsey in the melee and ran to him.

"Please!" she said, pushing Jeremy into his arms. "Take my baby to a paramedic and make sure he's all right. Drew's in the day care with my uncle and I've got to…"

"Whoa!"

She had turned to run toward the building and was completely shocked and deliriously happy when she collided with Drew. She threw her arms around him and let herself expel the scream she'd been holding since they'd run for the stairwell.

Then Drew turned her around again and pointed to two police officers leading her uncle away. "All taken care of," he said. He then pointed to the day care, where there was no sign of flames.

"He set the fire in the mudroom," Drew explained, "and fortunately all the fireproofing regs Katherine studiously followed pretty much confined it there and in the kitchen. Part of the floor in the mudroom gave way, though, and the floor fell through to the basement, which smoked up the tunnel."

She turned to throw her arms around him once

again. "Thank God you're okay. I had visions of it all going bad because I wouldn't be able to get there in time for you like you did for me."

JARON MET Drew's eye over Julia's head, a grin forming on his lips. "Glad to see you've finally found a good woman to protect you."

Drew returned his grin, accepting his fate. He might want to be the man in charge of this relationship, but he'd fallen in love with a woman of action. "No shortage of those in my life. Something else I'm going to have to live with."

Jaron looked confused. "Pardon me?"

"Long story," Drew replied. "Give me the baby. I'll take him to the paramedics myself."

Jaron held up Jeremy, who'd stopped crying and was watching the lights and action with wide eyes. "Good idea. But he looks fine to me. Thanks for catching Stanton. Nice of you to do my job."

Drew dismissed his praise as he took the baby. "Happy to oblige. Thanks for getting here so fast."

The paramedic checked Jeremy over in the back of the ambulance and declared him perfectly healthy. Then Helen and Katherine appeared, looking a little thrown together.

"Jaron called," Helen said. "Are you all right? Is Jeremy okay? Julia?"

"We're all fine," Drew assured her, handing her Jeremy to prove it.

"Katherine, I'm so sorry." Julia put her arms around Drew's sister. "I'll do whatever I can to help you. We'll hire the best people to repair and redecorate and pay them a bonus to do it quickly.''

Katherine shook her head. She looked weary, but her concern seemed to be for them, rather than the building. ''Actually, the damage is minimal, all things considered. I'm thinking if I got a work party together, called in a few favors, we could be open Monday morning. I'm just so grateful none of you is hurt.''

Drew turned to Julia. ''You realize, of course, that *we're* part of the work party and the few favors.''

''I do. Least we can do for a bridesmaid.''

''What?'' Katherine and Helen gasped simultaneously.

''We're getting married,'' Julia said, ''and moving to my house on the lake. With all the new families you signed up tonight, you're going to need the third floor.''

''Well, that's a disappointment,'' Katherine said grimly.

Drew frowned in surprise. ''You're not pleased we're getting married?''

''Oh, no, I like that part,'' she said with a devilish smile. ''But I was looking forward to having to throw you out when I expanded.''

Turning to his mother, Drew pointed at Katherine. ''See? You're always blaming me for our squabbles, but she's the one who starts them.''

''Tattletale,'' Katherine accused.

Helen, still holding Jeremy, rocked him in her arms as he dozed off. She ignored her children and said to Julia, ''I guess you three will have to come home with me for tonight,'' she said. ''It's going to take a while to clean up that smoke.''

Drew squeezed her shoulders. ''Thanks, Mom.''

As Drew led Julia in his mother's wake, she looked over her shoulder and saw the bearded man who'd walked through the tunnel with her. He was standing aimlessly in the middle of the confusion still reigning on Sandringham Drive.

Just as she was wondering what to do for him, a man in a clerical collar approached him. After exchanging a few words with him, the priest led him away.

She felt considerable relief, knowing he was probably being guided toward a shelter.

Drew and Katherine continued to squabble teasingly and Helen rolled her eyes at Julia. ''You're sure you want into this family?''

''Even if I have to pay dues,'' Julia replied, ''and wear a funny hat.''

FORRESTER SQUARE,
a new Harlequin series,
continues in September 2003 with
TWICE AND FOR ALWAYS
by Cathy Gillen Thacker…

When Meg Bassett and Brody Taylor divorced,
their fraternal twins were just infants. Brody was
about to move to Ireland, and joint custody would
have only created upheaval in their children's lives.
So Meg and Brody each took a twin…and they became single parents. It was a big mistake.

Five years later Meg moved to Seattle, unaware
that Brody had just moved there, too—and that both
twins were enrolled at Forrester Square Day Care!
How to tell the kids their new best friend was their
sibling? And how to tell each other they were still in
love?

Here's a preview!

CHAPTER ONE

A RAP SOUNDED at the door, and Katherine Kinard walked in, a twin on either side of her. For a moment Meg couldn't breathe. She'd seen pictures of Kevin, charting his progress as he grew from infant to toddler to little boy, but nothing had prepared her for the impact of seeing her child in person after five long years. He was so incredibly cute she couldn't take her eyes off him. And his twin sister, Kelly, was just as adorable.

"We're sorry," Kelly said.

"Yeah, we are," Kevin added earnestly in his sweet Irish accent.

"We didn't mean to mix up the beepers." Kelly bobbed up and down, unable to stand still, even for a second. Intent on talking them out of trouble, she failed to notice the tears Meg was blinking back and instead focused on Brody, who, Meg noted, was struggling to control his emotional reaction to seeing Kelly.

"I was just showing Mommy's beeper to Kevin this morning." Then Kelly pointed to Brody. "You were out in the yard and Mommy was talking to that other lady. Mommy's going to be our new music teacher," she finished proudly.

Meg drew a shaky breath. It was all she could do not to gather her little boy into her arms and hug him to her chest. But given the fact he still didn't have a clue who she really was...

"You're teaching here, too?" Brody's brow rose.

Meg swallowed hard around the lump of emotion in her throat. "Part-time, to the older classes, in exchange for reduced tuition for Kelly." Since she'd recently bought a small cozy home in Seattle after forgoing a paycheck for most of the summer, her finances were tight. "I start later this week."

"And then my daddy came back in, and we put the beepers back in his briefcase and your purse and we got 'em mixed up." Kevin continued his explanation with an exuberant array of hand and arm motions.

"We won't do it again," Kelly promised, an angelic expression on her face, "'cause we know beepers aren't a toy. Right, Kevin?" She elbowed her brother dramatically.

Kevin nodded vigorously in response.

So, Meg thought a little shakily as she slid the correct beeper back into her purse, that much was settled. As for the rest... With a heart that was filled to overflowing she looked at the child she had given up shortly after birth. What were she and Brody going to do? She was still precariously close to tears, wanting to take her little boy in her arms and hold him tight, yet knowing that would scare him. The overwhelming love and joy pouring out of her heart made it hard for her to hold on to her composure.

Meanwhile, Brody—who seemed to be struggling

with the same feelings as Meg—finally tore his eyes from Kelly and looked back at Meg. His dark eyes were glimmering with tears. ''I don't know about you,'' he said in a low, husky tone that seemed to come straight from his soul, ''but I'm thinking it might be a good idea to leave early for the day and go somewhere and talk.''

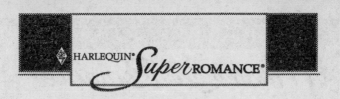

HARLEQUIN *Presents*

**The world's bestselling romance series...
The series that brings you your favorite authors,
month after month:**

Helen Bianchin...Emma Darcy
Lynne Graham...Penny Jordan
Miranda Lee...Sandra Marton
Anne Mather...Carole Mortimer
Susan Napier...Michelle Reid

and many more uniquely talented authors!

Wealthy, powerful, gorgeous men...
Women who have feelings just like your own...
The stories you love, set in exotic, glamorous locations...

HARLEQUIN *Presents*

Seduction and passion guaranteed!

HARLEQUIN®
INTRIGUE

WE'LL LEAVE YOU BREATHLESS!

If you've been looking for thrilling tales of
contemporary passion and sensuous love stories
with taut, edge-of-the-seat suspense—then
you'll love Harlequin Intrigue!

Every month, you'll meet four new heroes
who are guaranteed to make your spine tingle
and your pulse pound. With them you'll enter
into the exciting world of Harlequin Intrigue—
where your life is on the line
and so is your heart!

THAT'S INTRIGUE—
ROMANTIC SUSPENSE
AT ITS BEST!

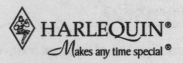

HARLEQUIN®
Makes any time special ®